DEADMAN'S
CASTLE

DEADMAN'S CASTLE

CASTLE

IAIN LAWRENCE

MARGARET FERGUSON BOOKS
HOLIDAY HOUSE · NEW YORK

Margaret Ferguson Books
Copyright © 2021 by Iain Lawrence
All Rights Reserved
HOLIDAY HOUSE is registered in the U.S. Patent and Trademark Office.
Printed and bound in January 2021 at Maple Press, York, PA, USA.
www.holidayhouse.com
First Edition
1 3 5 7 9 10 8 6 4 2

Library of Congress Cataloging-in-Publication Data

Names: Lawrence, Iain, 1955– author.
Title: Deadman's Castle / Iain Lawrence.
Description: New York : Margaret Ferguson Books, Holiday House, [2021]
Audience: Ages 9–12. | Audience: Grades 4–6. | Summary: "12-year-old
Igor and his family have been on the run from the sinister figure he
calls The Lizard Man for as long as he can remember and he wishes that
they could just live a normal life"—Provided by publisher.
Identifiers: LCCN 2020013114 | ISBN 9780823446551 (hardcover)
Subjects: CYAC: Witness protection programs—Fiction. | Family
life—Fiction. | Friendship—Fiction. | Middle schools—Fiction.
Schools—Fiction.
Classification: LCC PZ7.L43545 De 2021 | DDC [Fic]—dc23
LC record available at https://lccn.loc.gov/2020013114

ISBN: 978-0-8234-4655-1 (hardcover)

FOR
HAROLD STETLER

DEADMAN'S CASTLE

THE POLICEMAN

The policeman looked like a grizzly bear. He had little black eyes and a nose like a snout, and shoulders as wide as the doorway. He had to squeeze sideways into the kitchen, carrying a long gun that he placed carefully on the table. Then he sat down beside it, took off his hat, and didn't move until morning.

He came again the next day, and every day through all of November, always arriving just before dark. Nobody told me why he was there. But as a boy only five years old—a kid in kindergarten—I was thrilled to have a policeman in the house. I stared at his badge and his gun, hoping he would invite me to touch them. But he spoke to me only once, in a bearlike growl as I went up to bed. "Sleep tight, kid," he told me. "Don't let the bedbugs bite."

We moved away at the end of the month. I didn't know why. We went in such a hurry that I couldn't say goodbye to my friends, so suddenly that we left nearly everything behind, including—I imagined—the policeman. Months later, I still pictured him sitting all alone through the night in our kitchen.

We drove for many days, over mountains and prairies, to a little green house that smelled of cats. On our first night there, my father sat me down and said, "We need to have a talk."

I thought I was in trouble. On a creaky old sofa that was fuzzy with cat hair, I cuddled up beside Mom.

"We think it's time you learned a few things," said Dad. He stood in front of us, looking down. "A few months ago now, I saw someone do a terrible thing. So I went to the police and—"

"What did you see?" I asked.

"Shh," said Mom. She put her arm around me.

Dad started again. "I went to the police and told them what I saw. And now there's a very bad man coming after us."

"Why?"

"He wants to get even."

Mom pulled me closer, like she was trying to protect me. The springs in the sofa made squealing sounds.

Dad kept talking. "He'll try to find out where we live, and if he does . . ."

Dad never finished that sentence. He saw that I was nearly in tears and started over, maybe hoping not to scare me. "From now on," he said, "I want you to keep your eyes peeled. Watch for a man with a lizard tattooed on his skin."

"What do I do if I see him?" I asked.

"Run away," said Dad. "Scream for help. Do whatever it takes, but never let him catch you."

We changed our names and started over as a new family. Then, just as I was getting used to that, we moved again—and then again, and again. Wherever we went, that bad man was close behind us, and year after year we ran like rabbits in a field, dashing here and there, always in a panic. He chased us from Oregon to Florida, from Iowa to Idaho.

I imagined him in a thousand ways: now with the lizard clinging to his shoulder, a green tail coiled round his neck.

Now with a painted Godzilla standing in flames on his chest. Sometimes his whole body was one giant tattoo, with green scales all over him. And sometimes he was more a monster than a man, a slithering thing with claws instead of fingers.

I called him the Lizard Man, and for six years I lived in fear of him. Every night I dreaded going to sleep, because he even chased me in my dreams.

BUGGING OUT

On my twelfth birthday, when I leaned forward to blow out the candles on my cake, I actually wished for the Lizard Man to find us. I wanted it all to end, one way or the other. The flames bent and stretched like they didn't want to go out. But they did, and my little sister laughed and my parents clapped, and I saw all of us sitting there in our stupid paper hats and thought I might cry.

I hadn't had a real party, or even a friend, since kindergarten. I had moved so many times that I couldn't remember how many houses I'd lived in. And to top it all off, as I lay in bed that night trying not to sleep, I suddenly realized that I'd forgotten my real name.

It was a very cold night in the first days of winter. Through a tiny gap in the curtains I watched the bare branches of our chestnut tree moving in the wind. Like skinny witch's fingers, they clawed at the side of the house. They tapped on the glass. With blankets pulled up to my chin, I kept staring out through that gap as I worked backward through my list of names.

Alan Hess. Jordan Taylor. Darryl Edwards.

Some seemed like old friends I'd left behind. Others were more like strangers because I'd known them for only a few months, or a few weeks, or even a few days sometimes.

Gordon Labella. Bobby Bates.

4

I wanted very badly to get right to the end, or actually right to the beginning, back to the time when I'd never heard of the Lizard Man. But I fell asleep at some point, and the next thing I knew someone was leaning over me, pushing me down on the bed.

I tried to scream. A hand clamped over my mouth. I tried to kick. I tried to punch. But the person pressed even harder.

Then I heard his voice—and it was my father's voice—telling me in a hoarse whisper to lie still, to be quiet. "Shh," he said.

I let my arms go limp, my legs go limp, and I lay like a dead man. Then Dad took his hand from my mouth and told me, "We're leaving."

His voice was trembling. He stood up and closed the curtains all the way across. "Get your kit and come downstairs," he said. "I'm going to get the car ready."

He walked away through the faint pool of yellow that the night-light splashed across my carpet, out to the dark hallway and down the stairs. My little sister appeared in the doorway, holding the scrap of red blanket she called her grumpy, though none of us knew why. She had it bunched in her fist while she sucked her thumb.

Behind her came Mom, carrying a bag in each hand. She leaned into my room and whispered so Bumble wouldn't hear. "Dad says he's found us."

I felt a tingle inside me. Had my birthday wish come true?

"Hurry," said Mom. She stuffed one of the bags under her arm, took my sister's hand, and told her as cheerfully as she could, "Let's go downstairs, Bumblebee."

I threw back my blankets and grabbed my clothes from the floor, everything except my socks. I always slept in my socks. Automatically, I checked to make sure my emergency money was folded inside. My lifeline, Dad called it.

As I pulled on my pants, I heard a creak of wood from the hallway. It was the sort of noise the house made all the time, but I thought about how I was now alone upstairs and my imagination went a little crazy. I pictured the Lizard Man hiding in my closet, watching me through the slits in the louvered panel, and I was afraid he would come leaping out at me.

Slowly, I turned the handle. Then I yanked the door open, snatched my old Nike bag from the floor, and backed away. I stuffed my schoolwork inside it and hurried downstairs.

On the bottom step, my mom and my sister were cuddled together. Bumble had pinned a plastic barrette in her hair, a yellow duck with black eyes that jiggled as she looked up. "We're bugging out," she said.

That was my father's expression. He liked to talk like a soldier leading a raid or something. "We're good to go." "We're bugging out." It sounded better than "fleeing into the night" or "running away and starting over again." Poor Bumble still thought this was just the normal way of living. She had been doing it all her life and never wondered why.

Dad had turned on just enough lights that he could see his way through the house. It was so quiet that I could hear the tiny ticking of the clock. Five minutes to three. I went to the window beside the front door and peered between the curtains.

"You shouldn't do that!" yelled Bumble, knowing the rules. "Mom, he shouldn't do that!"

"Yes, come away from there," said Mom. But I pretended not to hear. If the Lizard Man was out there, I wanted to see him. I imagined him standing boldly on the sidewalk, in the cone of yellow light that fell from the streetlamp, with his shadow splotched on the pavement. But no one was there.

I had never seen the Lizard Man. Neither had my mom. It was always Dad who knew he was watching us, who found his footprints in wet grass or heard him creeping past our curtained windows.

In the garage, the car's trunk closed with an echoing whump. A moment later, Dad came up through the kitchen.

"Let's roll," he said.

Mom tucked Bumble under her arm like a little bird, and they went running down the three steps to the garage. I picked up my gym bag. Dad ushered me through the kitchen and down to the car. He shoved me through the back door, onto the floor beside Bumble, and covered us both with a blanket.

As always, he went back into the house one more time. Maybe, in a crazy way, he felt he had to make sure the stove was turned off. Or maybe he just had to be the last to leave, like the captain of his sinking ship. In a minute he was back, panting as he slid into the driver's seat. He locked the doors and started the engine.

I heard the garage door thump. Like a castle's drawbridge, it rumbled open. Dad backed out onto the street, switched into drive, and sped away from the house.

For half an hour he drove here and there, around corner after corner like a mouse running through a maze. For all I knew, there might have been a dozen cars racing after us. The only thing I could see was the floor. Then Dad stopped the car and sighed and said, "Okay. We're not being followed. I think we're safe."

Bumble and I popped out from under the blanket. Dad had parked in the bright gleam of lights at a 7-Eleven. In the window was a hot dog machine, with shriveled old dogs riding around and around like seniors on a Ferris wheel. The clerk—wearing a little paper hat—stared at us mindlessly through the red glow.

Dad went inside to use the pay phone. He had to report in to the people he called the Protectors, to tell them we were on the run again, so they could arrange for a new place to hide us. When he came back he cranked the car's heater up to high and started driving.

"Where are we going?" I asked.

He answered as he always did, with his favorite motto. "The less you know, the better."

WHAT THE MONKEY SAID

We each had our kit, our one bag that we kept packed and ready to go. Along with the stuff that Dad stored in the car, the bags held everything we needed to pass from one life into another. It was always funny to see what tiny thing Bumble added to hers after Mom had finished packing it. Once there was a rock; once there was a penny. This time it was a hardened piece of gum that she'd scraped off the sidewalk, thinking it was a diamond.

I had a few clothes and two pairs of shoes, and that was just about all I owned. I didn't have a computer, a cell phone, an iPad, or anything like that. Dad thought those things could be used to track us, so he banned them from our lives. The only thing he allowed was the spy phone. That was my name for Mom's fancy landline telephone that Dad had ordered from some shady place on the internet. It didn't show up on people's call displays, and it had a number that was not only unlisted, it didn't even exist. At least that's how Dad explained it. He was actually kind of proud of the spy phone. "The CIA would need at least two weeks to trace that thing," he'd told us.

Mom used it for her job. She was a telemarketer, selling ocean cruises to people too polite to hang up. Even as we worked our way east, zigzagging across the country, she kept making her calls. She plugged in that phone for an hour or two every evening at whatever motel Dad had chosen for the night and started dialing numbers. When somebody answered she shouted, "Ahoy there!" After a while it all seemed unreal, her voice repeating the same shtick in a different place that seemed a lot like the place before. I lost track of where we were. I lost track of time, and suddenly Mom didn't bother to plug in her phone one day.

It was Christmas Eve.

We were holed up in a room with orange walls and an orange carpet. The TV, the coffeemaker, and the microwave were chained to the wall.

"Well, it isn't much, but I guess it'll do," said Mom when Bumble had been put to bed in the other room. "I don't think anyone could *ever* find us here."

She didn't know how thin the walls were in that place. The bedroom door opened and Bumble came out. She shouted in her squeaky voice, "No one?"

"Not even Waldo," said Dad, which made no sense. He didn't always get his cultural references right.

My sister started crying. Mom sat beside her on the green sofa, pulled her close and asked, "What's the matter, Bumblebee?"

My sister kept wailing. "Santa Claus can't find us!"

I laughed—until Dad gave me a dirty look. "Oh, your mother's only kidding," he said. "I'm sure Santa has his ways."

It was like admitting there was a chink in the armor, that we weren't really all that safe after all. But Bumble didn't notice. Her tears vanished, and she was happy again.

I went to sleep hoping I would dream of Greenaway. It was a town that didn't exist, a cover story invented by Dad, to be told to anyone who asked where we came from. But in my dreams it had become a real place where kids played baseball in the sunset, where all the neighbors got together for backyard barbecues, and I would wake up believing for a moment that I was living there.

But that night I didn't dream at all.

In the morning a sad little pile of presents lay wrapped under the TV. There was a sweater for Mom and a tie for Dad, and for me a pair of huge snow boots with big dangling buckles. "Thanks," I said. "So this means we're not moving to Florida?" Bumble got the ugliest doll I'd ever seen, a mutant, googly-eyed monkey that might have escaped from a horror movie. I grimaced when I saw it, but my sister loved that thing. She carried it around everywhere she went and gave it the name of George. I called it Hideous George.

For Christmas dinner we ate a precooked chicken that came in a plastic dome, a tub of coleslaw, and little brown potatoes packed in a pouch like baby kangaroos. As we ate we watched TV, but we kept the sound turned down to a murmur so Dad could listen for footsteps and car engines.

Later, Bumble put Hideous George to bed. She tucked her grumpy around his chin, curled up beside him, and spent a long time whispering into his ear like he was actually talking back to her. When she turned toward us she looked very serious. "George wants to stay home next Christmas," she said.

"Oh, does he?" asked Mom.

Bumble nodded solemnly. "He doesn't like traveling around. He just wants to stay home."

It was pretty obvious she was talking about herself. But Mom and Dad pretended not to know that.

"I think George will be very happy when he gets settled into a new house," said Mom. "Who knows—he might have a tree in the backyard and a tire to swing on."

Bumble whispered that bit of news into the monkey's ear, then listened to his answer. "He says he's scared he'll have to bug out again," she said. "He wants to stay in one place forever."

"So do I," said Mom. "All of us would like to do that."

Dad was gazing down at the orange carpet, and he looked pretty miserable. Then Mom touched his arm and smiled at him. "I think it's time for George to go to sleep now."

That night, my parents argued. Their voices came through the skinny wall of the motel room, loud enough to wake me up. The first words I heard sounded a little crazy. It was Dad talking.

"So you're siding with the monkey?"

"Oh, don't be silly," said Mom.

"Well, really."

"I'm just saying I can't go on like this."

Dad was angry. "What's that supposed to mean?"

"I don't know," said Mom. "But I'm wearing out. I've—"

"Shhhh!" said Dad. "You'll wake them up."

Mom started whispering. Dad whispered back, and I couldn't make out another word of what they were saying, even when I pressed my ear right against the wall. I had heard

Mom complaining before about how hard it was to keep moving from place to place, about never having a real home. But this time felt different.

When I tried to go back to sleep, I couldn't. I lay on the hard bed, watching city lights shimmer on the curtains, and knew I'd still be watching them when the sun came up. I was used to *that,* all right. But it was a whole new fear that kept me awake in the orange room, something I'd never even thought about.

What if my parents broke up?

I worried about it so much that I talked to my mom the first chance I got, as we sat in the car at a gas station. Dad was working the pump. Bumble was "helping" him, gripping the hose in her tiny hands.

"Mom, are you going to leave us?"

She turned around, puzzled. "Leave you where?"

"You know. Are you going away on your own?"

She looked shocked. "No. Of course not," she said. "Why would you ask me that?"

"I heard you talking to Dad. You were fighting."

"We weren't *fighting,*" she said. "Sometimes I get tired of living this way, and I guess I take it out on your father. But wherever we go, we go together. I promise."

She reached into the backseat and touched my arm. "It's going to get better," she said. "I believe that."

"Well, it can't get any worse," I told her.

DEAD END

It usually took the Protectors only a couple of weeks to find us a place to live. But January came and went, and we were still traveling east. We had gone nearly all the way across the country when we suddenly turned around and headed west again. On the first day of February, we holed up in a dark motel called the Buena Vista. That means "good view," but all we could see was a snow-covered parking lot.

I didn't know why Mom seemed unusually nervous that night. She checked twice to make sure the door was properly locked. Every noise from outside made her look up and ask, "What was that?" Once it was a dog going by, panting on its leash. Another time, it was an ambulance wailing in the distance.

"Honey, calm down," Dad told her, which was pretty funny in a way. He'd always been the one listening for noises, always wondering who was outside.

The very next evening, he gave Bumble the talk.

She sat beside Mom on a sofa made of fake leather, her little legs sticking straight out in front of her. Dad paced back and forth. "In a few months you'll turn five," he said. "We think it's time you learned a few things."

He had used those same words in the house that smelled of cats, on the day when I had got the talk. But years had passed since then, and Dad looked a hundred years older. He had gray in his hair, deep lines on his forehead, and wrinkles around his mouth.

"A long time ago, before you were born," he told Bumble, "I went to the police about something I'd seen."

I felt sorry for poor little Bumble. Half smiling, she looked up at Dad with no idea what was coming next.

"I don't regret it," said Dad. "That was the right thing to do. But there was a very bad man who got angry. He said he would find me and get even. So that's why we keep moving, so the bad man won't catch us."

Bumble's face suddenly crinkled with worry. She clutched her grumpy and leaned against Mom.

"You'll know who he is if you see him," said Dad. "He has a lizard on his skin."

When I got the talk, that had been the moment when my life had changed forever. Not once ever since had I gone to sleep at night without first getting down on my knees to look under my bed. Dad had frightened me so badly that I wanted to yell at him now to shut up before he did the same thing to Bumble. But I only sat there and listened, just as I'd done as a little boy.

"We want you to watch for that man," said Dad. "But we don't want you to be afraid of him."

"*What?*" I couldn't believe I'd heard him right. But Dad ignored me.

"That man's not going to hurt *you*," he told Bumble. "Don't worry about that. But if you see him, you have to tell me right away. You can tell your mom, or tell your brother, whoever's closest. But don't tell anyone else. Understand?"

Bumble nodded.

"We'll make it a game," said Dad. "Like I Spy. I spy with my little eye a man with a lizard on his skin."

That made Bumble giggle. It made *me* angry, everything I'd feared suddenly turned into a joke.

Bumble didn't seem at all upset when the talk was over. She hopped down from the sofa and turned on the TV. Dad looked pleased with himself. He said, "I think that went well."

Mom nodded but didn't say anything.

There was a sitcom on TV, fake laughter coming quietly from the speakers. I said, "So we don't have to be afraid of the Lizard Man anymore?"

"Of course we do," said Dad. "Weren't you even listening? Nothing's changed."

"But you told Bumble he's not going to hurt her. You said—"

"We don't want to scare her," said Mom. "We want her to be careful, not terrified."

I wished they had thought of that when *I* got the talk. It made me jealous of Bumble.

"The danger's real," said Dad, keeping his voice very low. "Don't think that monster's not still after us."

I had a bad dream that night. I was running from a man who would not stop chasing me. He leapt over hedges, over fences, bounding along through the dark.

Mom heard me screaming. She came to see what was wrong and found me tangled in my blankets, covered in sweat. She sat down beside me and held me until I woke.

"It's okay. It's okay," she kept saying. "We're safe."

But she didn't act as though we were safe. There was something about that place that made Mom a nervous wreck. When Dad went out alone each morning to take care of the business of starting over, she wedged a chair under the doorknob. Every night, she asked Dad: "When are we getting out of here?"

I wasn't allowed to leave the room alone. But I could understand that. I had such a lousy sense of direction I might not have found my way back. So I stayed in the room with Mom and Bumble and did hours of schoolwork. I watched TV with Bumble, or just enjoyed the *buena vista* through the slits of the venetian blinds, watching cars come and go in the parking lot.

We had been trapped in that room for nearly two weeks when Dad came back to the motel at noon one day. He used our secret knock to let us know it was him: three quick taps, a pause, and then three more. Mom got up to let him in. When she opened the door he was standing there with a silver chain dangling from his fingers. On the end of it hung a key.

"Anyone want to go see our new house?" he asked.

Bumble bounced on the bed, shrieking happily. "What color is it, Dad?"

He shrugged. "I guess we'll have to wait and see." It was a tradition that we always went together to a new place.

"I hope it's yellow!" shouted Bumble. She had always hoped for a yellow house and had always been disappointed.

"I hope it has a swimming pool," I said.

"I hope it's *safe*," said Mom.

I put on my new snow boots, Mom put on a coat, and all of us stuffed Bumble into her pink snowsuit as she giggled and squirmed. Then off we went to see our house.

It was a cold day with fresh snow that sparkled in the sunlight. Strapped in her car seat, Bumble wore enormous green sunglasses that made her look like a giant bug. In five minutes she was fast asleep. In another five so was I, and both of us missed the ride across the city. I woke as the car went over a bump on a concrete bridge and my head smacked against the window.

There was a river below me, though not very wide. Even my mom could have skipped a stone across it, and she was even worse than me at skipping stones. Nearly frozen right over, it had one channel of dark water flowing down the middle like a blood vein.

"Where are we?" I asked.

Nobody answered. I felt like Rip Van Winkle, suddenly awake in a world where everything had changed. Mom was so upset that I could *feel* it, and Dad held the steering wheel in a death grip as he stared grimly through the windshield. I wondered what had happened to make them angry at each other.

The car rumbled over the concrete bridge. We passed a riverside park where trees glistened like silver ornaments. Then Dad slowed the car and turned right. "I guess this is our street," he said.

On the corner was a yellow sign: DEAD END ROAD. I said, "Wouldn't it be funny if that was the name of the street?"

To our left were town houses, one after the other, as square and plain as the buildings on a Monopoly board. To our right was the park, a strip of bushes and trees along the riverbank. With everything frosty and bright, it looked beautiful, but Mom stared straight ahead as Dad drove slowly along.

This was the only part about bugging out that I actually enjoyed. I loved driving down a strange street to see a new house. It was always a bit exciting, a bit scary, a bit sad somehow. Usually, we would babble away, everybody talking at the same time, making guesses about what we would find. This time, the car stayed chillingly silent.

"What's the address?" I asked.

"Thirty-eight," said Dad.

The end of the street was already in sight. Three tall apartment buildings lined a cul-de-sac, and it looked like we were going to be living in one of them. That was a big disappointment. I didn't want to be sealed in a place with a balcony for a backyard. Apartments were prisons.

Mom felt the same way. In an icy voice she said, "I was hoping to live in a nice little house."

"Just wait," snapped Dad.

I couldn't imagine why he thought he might find a house on that street. But as we passed a tangle of bushes and trees at the end of the park, one suddenly appeared. It was a big old yellow house squashed between the park and the first towering apartment building. There were no footprints on its snowy lawn, no tire tracks in the driveway. It was like a little fairy-tale castle created by magic just for us.

"And here we are," said Dad as he pulled into the driveway. "What do you think?"

I loved it. Right away it was my favorite of all the houses I could remember. There was no swimming pool, but I wasn't surprised. Instead, we had the park beside us, and a river in our backyard, and on the far side of the river, a forest so thick and dark that I could imagine it full of wild animals.

Dad called over his shoulder. "Do you like it, Bumblebee?"

I nudged her. Like always, she went in an instant from sound asleep to wide awake. She turned to the window, grinned, and shouted, "It *is* yellow! It's like a giant dollhouse."

Only Mom wasn't happy. She sat with her arms crossed, as stiff as a corpse.

"Don't you like it, Mom?" I asked.

"It's asking for trouble," she said.

"Why?"

"Ask your father."

I didn't waste my breath. "Well, I'm going to go see it," I said. "Come on, Bumble."

"No!" shouted Mom, swiveling around in her seat.

I had the door open, my foot stuck out in the cold. "What's wrong?" I asked.

"I don't want you going down to that river," she said. "Not by yourselves. Not ever."

So that was the problem. Mom was afraid of the river.

"Mom, it's not dangerous," I told her. "It's just a little river."

"That doesn't matter." She glared at me, and then at Bumble. "You promise me right now—both of you—that you'll never walk out on the ice."

"All right," I said. "No problem."

Bumble smiled. "No problem."

"Well, okay then," said Dad, like everything was suddenly just fine. "Let's *all* have a look inside."

The house was so old that it had a mail slot in the front door. Bumble pried it open and peered inside as Dad worked the lock. Then he turned the key and we burst into that house like home invaders. I raced upstairs and claimed the corner bedroom at the back, with a window looking over the river and another looking over the park. If we were still in the house when the snow melted, I would be able to climb out onto the roof of a small back porch. It was slanted, covered with a tangled mat of ivy vines, but I didn't mind. I could see myself sitting there in summer sunshine, watching the river go by.

Bumble got the room next to mine, and Mom and Dad were way down the hall at the front of the house.

That same day, we checked out of the motel and settled in at our new place. After spending weeks in little motel rooms we felt like we'd come to a mansion. I thought it was great until I went up to bed on the first night. The stairs creaked under my feet; the hallway yawned darkly in front of me; cold air blasted from my room when I opened the door.

Just then, I didn't feel at home at all. My room was furnished like a jail cell, with a narrow bed under the window, a small dresser, and one empty shelf. I sat cross-legged on my bed, opened a crack in the curtains, and looked out toward the river. On my left, the huge wall of the apartment building next door towered over the house. Some of the windows were lit up, and others were dark, and they made an enormous, glowing checkerboard on the snowy lawn in front of me. Everything else was utterly black. There was not a single light on the other side of the river.

My fear of the Lizard Man rushed over me as strong as ever. Was he out there, hidden by shadows, watching the house?

I got up and turned out the lights. And then, in complete darkness, I went back and looked again. Moonlight glimmered on the river, reflecting off the ice and that vein of black water.

I told myself it was impossible that the Lizard Man was there. He had never found us on the first day. Twice my father had heard him prowling around a new house in the first week. And in the first month . . . Well, that had happened more times than I wanted to think about.

All night I stared out through the window. I didn't sleep until dawn.

BECOMING THE WATSONS

We settled in to start over again. Like always, we got new names to begin our new lives. Dad became Michael Watson; Mom became Sophie. My sister got the name Willow, though it made no difference. She would always be Bumble to us. I was tired of being given new names, like a dog being passed from owner to owner, so I asked to choose my own for once. Dad automatically said no, but after thinking about it for a while he said, "Oh, why not."

I had spent years waiting for that moment. I had gone through a million choices and picked out the one name I thought was perfect.

"No," said Dad when I told him.

"Why not? It's cool."

"No, it is not 'cool,'" he said. "It's stupid. People will laugh at you."

"But you said—"

"Oh, all right!" He did a flapping thing with his hands, like he was trying to fling them off the ends of his arms. "Call yourself whatever you want; I don't care."

So I became Igor.

But Dad wasn't finished with me. "At least pick a middle name," he said.

"I already did. It's—"

"A *normal* middle name. So you have something to fall back on when you come to your senses."

On that day my past was erased yet again. Everything I'd known and everything I'd done was left behind like an old scrapbook tossed in the garbage. I began life all over as Igor Andrew Watson.

But that was just the beginning. Every time we changed lives we changed cars. For as long as I could remember we had driven around in brown hatchbacks and gray sedans that nobody would ever notice. This time, Dad came home in a bright green minivan. Out in the driveway, it looked like a giant jelly bean. I wondered if the Protectors had let Dad choose his own car like I had chosen my name. Maybe he figured six seats would make bugging out more comfortable. But one of Mom's weird superstitions said green cars were unlucky, and she told Dad to "take that thing back right now."

"I can't," said Dad. "It's all settled."

Mom said the same thing about the car that she'd said about the house. "This is asking for trouble."

The only one who liked that minivan was Bumble. "Can we go for a drive?" she asked.

"That's a great idea," said Dad.

"Now?" cried Mom. "It's almost dark."

"What are you talking about?" said Dad. "It's a beautiful afternoon."

Sometimes they couldn't agree on anything, but this time both of them were right. Outside, everything seemed cold and gloomy—until the moment we pulled out of the driveway and passed from the shadows of the apartment buildings into dazzling sunlight. It didn't seem too bright in the back because the windows were heavily tinted. But Dad, in the front, turned his head like he'd been struck by a death ray. He lowered his visor to shield himself, and I saw all his slips of paper carefully clipped in place, his emergency phone numbers, his checklists. He moved them from car to car, always ready for the Lizard Man to put us on the run again.

We drove up Dead End Road, past the town houses, to the busy street with the concrete bridge. But instead of turning left and crossing the river, Dad turned right.

"This is Jefferson Street," he said, like none of us could read road signs. It was lined by stores and coffee shops, and groups of people—bundled up against the cold—strolled along in the sunshine. On the next corner was a little grocery store with bins of vegetables out on the sidewalk. Old women in shaggy coats grazed among them like a herd of wild ponies.

Dad turned right again, onto Thirty-First Avenue. "This is going to be our neighborhood," he said. "It's called the Horseshoe because the river wraps around it in a big loop. You'll see what I mean."

The numbered avenues ran north to south. The cross streets were all named after presidents. Dad drove along every one of them, back and forth, up and down, meeting the river again and again. Mom seemed really nervous at first, but on Van Buren Street she started relaxing. On Harding she nodded and smiled. "I think we'll be okay," she said.

I loved the neighborhood. Towering trees lined the streets, reaching out with their bare winter branches to touch each other high above us. There were old-fashioned houses with little windows and big porches, painted every color you'd find in a box of crayons. We passed a public swimming pool, a baseball diamond, a playground with a sandbox, and a tiny pond. Mom kept saying, "Isn't that lovely."

Then we found the school.

It was a big square of red brick and white windows. We came at it from the back, around a football field where the wind whipped little clouds of snow into sparkling spirals. At the front entrance a sign said RUTHERFORD B. HAYES MIDDLE SCHOOL. Behind a row of flagpoles, wide stairs climbed to the front doors. At the bottom, one on each side, a pair of concrete lions crouched on tall pillars.

Classes had just finished. Kids were pouring out from the school, spreading in every direction like gumballs spilled from a big dispenser. They rolled through the gates, over the sidewalk, out across the street in front of us. Dad stopped the car to let them cross.

A group of kids my own age, or pretty close, were gathering around one of the lions. In the cold air they spouted tiny clouds of breath as they laughed and talked.

Seeing them made me feel lonely. I hadn't been inside a school since my time in kindergarten, and I could barely remember that. I wished I could be one of them, a normal kid who would sleep over at a friend's house, or talk to a girl who wasn't my mom, or play catch with a guy who wasn't my dad.

A girl in a black coat and black boots scrambled onto one of the pillars and sat astride the concrete lion at the top. She leaned on its neck and drummed her heels on its flanks, like she was riding that thing through the sky.

The street cleared of kids, a couple of stragglers went by, and Dad starting driving. He passed the school, turned onto another street, and went around and around through the Horseshoe until I had no idea where we were. Poor Bumble went to sleep again, and as we neared Jefferson for the ump-teenth time, Mom got impatient. "I think we should go back," she said. "I've had enough."

Dad turned the car and headed home to Dead End Road.

DAD'S RULES

I lived inside an invisible fence. Dad built a new one around every house, setting down rules that told me how far I could go in any direction, and where I couldn't go at all. On the night after our drive, when Bumble had gone to bed, he sat with Mom and me and drew out my boundaries.

"I'm only going to make three rules," he said, which made me hopeful for a moment. But my heart fell as he checked them off on his fingers. "Stay on this side of the river. Always be home before dark. Never cross Jefferson."

"But, Dad—"

He held up his hand. "No arguments."

The three rules locked me into the smallest cage I'd ever had. I was stuck in the Horseshoe, in that bend of the river on the south side of Jefferson. It was a space I could cross in less than an hour.

"I can see you're disappointed," said Dad. "But right now we have to be more careful than ever. You have to watch for anything suspicious."

He named those things I had to watch for, and his list seemed almost endless: old men in big cars, young men in black cars, any cars with tinted windows and shadowy figures inside. He told me to watch for men with long coats, for men with short hair, for men with thick necks and dark glasses and shiny black shoes. He told me to watch for anything unusual. It seemed the years that had passed had made him more afraid. Or afraid of more things.

That was on Friday. I barely spoke to Dad that whole weekend. First thing on Monday morning, he went out— just like a normal person going off to a job. Bumble didn't want him to go. After living so close together in different motels, she didn't like to see us apart. She sat on his foot with her arms around his leg, laughing like it was just a game. "You have to stay home!" she shouted. "I'm not going to let you go."

"I'll be back before you know it," said Dad. "Don't worry, Bumble." Then he gave his usual orders to Mom. "Lock the door behind me. Throw the dead bolt and put the chain on the latch. Don't let anyone in. And keep the curtains closed."

As soon as he was gone, Mom set up her spy phone in the kitchen. She connected the headset and arranged her pads of paper.

Bumble climbed up on a chair to sit beside her. She would spend the morning with coloring books, believing she was working.

"Mom?" I said. "Why is Dad such a loser?"

Mom looked shocked. "What an awful thing to say. You used to worship your father."

Well, he wasn't *always* a loser. In the years before the Lizard Man, Dad had been a university professor, teaching English literature. But I had no memory of that. For as long as *I* could remember, Dad had never had a job. He either hung around the house reading books or went out to do mysterious things that he never talked about.

Mom plugged the spy phone into the wall jack. "You don't know half of what goes on around here," she said.

"Well, no wonder. Nobody tells me anything."

"And that's for your own good," she said, and I laughed because she sounded *exactly* like Dad.

Mom clamped her headset over her ears and made her first call. Through the tiny speakers I heard a phone ringing. Someone answered, said hello.

"Ahoy there!" shouted Mom.

I sailed up to my room and did schoolwork until two o'clock crawled around. Then I packed up my books, put them away, and went back down to the kitchen. I told Mom, "I'm going out."

She glanced up from the spy phone. "Where are you going?"

"Just out."

She looked worried. "Do you think you could be happy playing in the yard?"

"I'm not going out to *play*," I told her. "I'm not a little kid, Mom."

I turned to leave. From behind me came Bumble's quiet voice. "What if the bad man gets him?"

She didn't sound afraid. She was just curious, and I found that kind of creepy. When I looked back I saw her bent over her coloring book, holding her hair out of her eyes as she scribbled away with a red crayon.

"The bad man's not going to get him," said Mom. "That bad man's not going to get *anybody*."

"How do you know?" asked Bumble.

"Because your father says so."

That didn't make me feel any safer. Bumble switched to a yellow crayon and asked in that same calm way, "Do you think the bad man's hiding somewhere?"

"Bumble, please," said Mom. "Your father made the rules, and we have to trust him. Everything will be all right if we do what he says."

A little spooked by the whole thing, I said, "Maybe I'll just stay home."

"No," said Mom. "You don't have to do that." She took off her headset and put it down on the table. "Come on. I'll let you out."

She stood up to walk me to the door.

"Goodbye, Igor," said Bumble, like I might never come back.

In the hall I put on my coat and my boots. I took the chain from the latch, turned the dead bolt, and opened the door. In that moment, as I looked out, I saw the world as I imagined my dad must see it all the time, every shadow a lurking man.

"Go ahead; it's all right," said Mom. "Just be careful."

I felt like a baby bird being pushed from the nest. If I didn't start flying, I'd fall flat on my face.

"Don't get lost," said Mom as I stepped through the door. "Stay away from the river and don't cross Jefferson."

I couldn't possibly stop and go back. So I strode out of the house and down the steps like I didn't have a fear in the world. I heard my mom close the door behind me. I heard the dead bolt click.

Bumble had scared me. At the end of the driveway I stopped and looked around for the Lizard Man. I peered into the bushes of the riverside park, then up at the apartments next door. Though I was alone on the street, I imagined that I was being watched by hundreds of people gazing from their windows. That made me feel safer, and I started walking in the only direction I could—north toward Jefferson Street.

When I reached the corner I stood there and gawked at the cars going by. I didn't understand Dad's rule about crossing Jefferson. It wasn't like a different world lay waiting on the other side. Dead End Road kept on going and it looked just the same over there. But to be told *not* to cross the street made me wonder where it went and, again, why Dad didn't want me to find out. It was like getting a present and being told not to open it. So you shake it and poke it, and you start pulling at the wrapping paper, and then you can't stop until you've finally seen inside.

I knew that one day I would cross Jefferson and see where Dead End Road would take me. But I didn't do it then. I was still just a kid afraid of the Lizard Man, a kid who did what he was told. I turned right on Jefferson instead, and right again one block later, following the route through the president streets that Dad had taken us on in the jelly bean car.

I didn't go looking for the school. I couldn't have found it if I'd tried. But that was where I ended up. I turned a corner and the entrance was right in front of me. So I leaned on the fence and watched the windows like they were movie screens at a multiplex. Seeing the kids in the classrooms made me remember things: the smell of Elmer's glue, the snicking of scissors, the rough-smooth feel of construction paper. I kind of traveled back in time as I stood there, and it made me jump when buzzers blasted inside the school. Every window was suddenly an action movie, with kids swarming everywhere. In a moment they came boiling through the doors like bats from a cave.

The same kids I'd seen before gathered around the concrete lion. Soon a dozen were standing there, talking in loud voices. I watched for a while, then started back toward the yellow house, knowing what I wanted to do.

FUN AND GAMES

The minivan was parked in the driveway, so I knew Dad had come home. I tapped our secret knock on the door and the mail slot opened. Bumble's tiny fingers appeared. Her voice squeaked through the gap. "Guess what? Dad got a job."

"Yeah, sure he did," I said.

"It's true!"

I heard Mom laughing, then the lock clicked and the door swung open, and she and Bumble were standing there with Hideous George squeezed in my sister's arm.

"What job did he get?" I asked.

"He hasn't told us yet," said Mom. "He only just came home."

I followed her through the house. On the kitchen table, the spy phone and Mom's papers had been pushed aside. Dad was sitting there, drinking coffee.

"So what job did you get?" I asked.

"Well, the job—per se—is not too exciting," he said. "I'll have to work some weekends, maybe a few holidays, but the hours are flexible. And the best thing is, it's close to home. I'll only be two blocks away."

"Isn't that incredible?" said Mom, with a huge smile. "What do you think, kids? Who else could go out for a few hours and land a job two blocks away? You should tell your father you're proud of him."

Dad said, "That's not necessary."

But Bumble leaned her head against him. "I'm proud of you, Dad," she said.

He patted her awkwardly, looking embarrassed. Actually, *I* would have looked embarrassed too, because it turned out Dad had found the crummiest job in the world. He would be handing out brochures on Jefferson Street for a company called Fun and Games. It put on theme parties for children and sold balloons and games and things.

Mom beamed at him. "You'll need a new suit!"

But Dad shook his head. "They give me something to wear."

"Like a uniform?" I asked.

"Sort of."

He obviously didn't want to talk about it. Bumble started showing him the pictures she'd drawn in her coloring book, and he acted like he was absolutely riveted. Soon she was laughing, and when Bumble laughed everybody laughed, because the sight of her was just so funny. For the first time in ages we were one happy family, and I saw my chance.

I said, "I want to go to school."

An awful silence fell over the room. Nobody looked at anybody else. Then Mom hurried around the table and took Bumble by the hand. "Let's play in the living room!" she said, whisking my sister away. Dad fiddled with his coffee cup, turning it in circles. He said, "I've been expecting this."

He had a theory, he said, that boys go a little crazy around the age of twelve. "For some it's a year sooner, and for some it's a year later, but it always happens," he said. "I wanted to build a raft and float down the Mississippi like Huckleberry Finn. *My* father wanted to be a soldier and fight in a war. *His* father wanted to drive a wagon train, and the last one had gone west long before he was even born."

"I just want to go to school," I said.

"Not really," said Dad. "You only *think* you do. Believe me, you wouldn't be happy in school."

"I was happy in kindergarten."

"Things are different now." Dad sat straighter in his chair. "Look, son."

He hardly ever called me son, and he had never talked so gently. He held out his hands like he wanted to touch me but drew them back again.

"The children in that school will have known each other all their lives," he said. "They'll have memories and experiences you could never share. You'd be a pariah."

"What's that?"

"An outcast." Dad picked up his empty cup and put it down again. "The truth is, you're as different from them as night is from day. You'd have nothing in common to bring you together."

"You just don't want me to have friends," I said.

"That's not true."

"You're afraid I'll tell them things, and they'll tell other people, and maybe the Lizard Man will hear about this kooky kid who's lived in a million houses and—"

"All right, yes," said Dad. "That scares me to death. But it's not that I don't *want* you to have friends. I just can't turn you loose into that sort of environment."

"I wouldn't tell anybody anything, Dad."

He smiled but somehow still looked sad. "Do you really think that's possible?"

"Sure. I'll tell them the Greenaway story." *Oh, it's just a little town, you wouldn't have heard of it. My dad had a hardware store.*

"And how far is that going to get you with people you see every day?" he asked. "You can't build friendships out of lies."

"But, Dad—"

"It's for your own good."

I was sick of being told that things were for my own good. What did that even mean? If it was for my own good, why didn't it make me happy?

"Believe me, I would love to send you to school," said Dad. "I'm a teacher, for heaven's sake. Or I was. When our circumstances change, the first thing I'll do is get you into a good school. I promise."

"When?"

"Maybe next year," he said. "If not, the one after. Almost certainly."

It seemed hopeless. I felt so sorry for myself that tears started leaking from my eyes. I squinted to stop them.

"Look." Dad sighed. "I know you hate me for this. But—"

"Dad, I don't hate you," I said. "You want to keep us safe. I get it, but..." There was no use trying to stop the tears anymore. They rolled down my cheeks and over my lips, warm and salty. "It's just so hard, Dad."

"It's hard on all of us, son."

Yeah, right, I thought.

"But it's probably harder on you than on anyone else. I know that, and I'm sorry." Dad held out his hands again, and this time he hugged me. I leaned against him, just like Bumble had done. Through his clothes and through his skin, I could feel my father's heart beating very fast.

FOLLOWED HOME

I saw Dad at work the next afternoon when I walked up to Jefferson. I turned the corner and there he was, standing on the crowded sidewalk just a few yards away, trying to push his brochures onto people who mostly ignored him.

I ducked into a doorway and peered at him around its edge. He was wearing a huge bow tie and a pair of patched-up pants ten sizes too big, held up by red suspenders. On his feet were enormous shoes, on his head a fuzzy wig of orange hair, on his face a bright red nose and a painted smile.

My dad was a clown.

It was awful to see him there, with that ghastly smile on his face. At first I felt embarrassed. But then it made me angry to think why he'd taken that lousy job. He had become a sentry in a clown suit, guarding the entrance to Dead End Road, making sure I couldn't go *anywhere* without being seen.

I hadn't broken any of his rules, but I didn't want him to see me just then. I didn't want him to guess where I was going. So I went back down Dead End Road to look for another way around, and I found it at the very end, right across from the house. Between the big apartment buildings and the little town houses was a path worn through the snow. It led to a walkway lined with planters and lampposts, and at the end was an iron gate. I passed through it, into the maze of streets named after presidents.

I was heading for Rutherford B. Hayes Middle School. But of course I couldn't find it, and for nearly an hour I wandered through the neighborhood. When I finally blundered onto the front entrance, I didn't loiter around the fence. I marched right up the path and past the lions, up the steps and into the school.

A big yellow sign told me ALL VISITORS MUST REPORT TO THE OFFICE. A painted arrow showed the way, past display cases full of photographs and trophies.

There must have been a thousand kids in that building. But they were all tucked away in their classrooms, and the building felt deserted. I walked down the empty hall with my boots squeaking on the floor, my buckles jingling like a gunfighter's spurs.

The office door was open. A lady stood at a counter stapling papers together. She tipped her head and looked down at me over the pearly frame of her glasses. The wrinkles around her mouth looked as hard as cement, like she hadn't smiled in thirty years.

"May I help you?" she said.

"I want to go to school," I told her.

She stopped stapling. "Are you trying to be funny, young man?"

"No," I said. "I want to go to school. I don't have to pay, do I?"

She stared at me a little longer. "Just a minute," she said, and walked away into another room.

In a moment she was back. She brought a younger lady

in a gray skirt, who smiled at me and said, "I'm Principal Harris. And you are...?"

"Igor."

She looked suspicious. "You don't go to school at all?"

"I get homeschooling," I told her. "But I want to come here instead."

"It's not that simple," she said. "You can't just walk into a school and start classes. You have to be registered by your parents. You need their approval."

"But they wouldn't approve," I told her. "Especially not my dad."

"Oh?" She raised her eyebrows. "Why is that?"

"He doesn't want me talking to people."

"Is that so?" Principal Harris frowned. "Hmmm," she said. "I think I'd better meet this father of yours."

It was about then that I understood why Dad didn't want me talking to people. Principal Harris invited me into her office, closed the door, and started asking questions. I started with the Greenaway story, but almost before I knew it I was giving her my address. To make things even worse, I realized I didn't know the name of the street. "It's Dead End Road," I said stupidly. "The street beside the river. With the big apartments."

The school day ended. With a sound like a buffalo stampede, the halls filled, then emptied. I wanted to leave too, but Principal Harris kept me there. Through her windows I saw the sky turning gray as she grilled me about my homeschooling. "My dad calls it 'unschooling,' I told her. "He gives me books and I write reports. He used to be a professor." Then she raised her eyebrows and said, "Oh, really? And he ran a hardware store in Greenaway?"

It was a nightmare. When I left her office the building really *was* deserted. I lost my way in the halls and went out through a back door. Afraid I might not make it home before dark, I started jogging. I aimed for the iron gate to Dead End Road but ended up on Jefferson Street.

People were moving along the sidewalk. They bunched up at the corners to wait for the lights, then burst across like flocks of startled birds. Fun and Games had closed for the day; Dad wasn't there. On Dead End Road, the town house windows lit up one by one as I hurried by. There was no more than half an hour of daylight left, and the little overgrown patch of bushes and trees at the end of the park seemed black and spooky.

I ran up the driveway, and Dad opened the front door as I stumbled onto the porch. "Where have you been?" he said. "A few minutes more and—"

He looked past me. A car was driving slowly up the street.

"Did that car follow you?" he asked.

"I don't think so," I said.

"You don't *think so?*" He grabbed my shoulder and hauled me into the house. Then he closed the door to a crack and peered through it.

I had an awful thought that Principal Harris had come for her talk with Dad. But the car went past our driveway at the same slow speed, with Dad watching every moment. He said, "I want to know where you've been."

I wasn't ready to tell him the truth, not when he was already angry. I said, "Just out."

"Did you talk to anybody?"

"Dad!"

He opened the door again and stepped out to look down the street. Standing behind him, I saw the car swing around in the loop. It came just as slowly back again. Then its headlights flashed across the trees as it turned into our driveway.

"SOMEONE'S GETTING OUT!"

I thought Dad would have a fit when he saw the car stop outside the house. He barged back across the porch, yelling at me to "Get inside!" I was already in the doorway, but he gave me a push that sent me reeling into the hall. Then he closed the door to a narrow slit again and pressed his eye against it.

"The headlights have turned off," he said. "I think he's found us."

I said, "Dad—"

"Get down!" He motioned toward the floor.

Mom came into the hall with Bumble half hiding behind her. "What's going on?" she asked.

"Keep back!" said Dad. "The car door's opening. Someone's getting out!"

"Who is it?" asked Mom.

"I can't see yet."

Mom spread out her arms to shield Bumble. I said, "Dad, it's not the Lizard Man."

He looked at me, his face so white that I could see the outline of his clown smile still circling his cheeks, the makeup not quite washed away. I said, "It's the principal from the school."

"How could you possibly know that?" he asked.

" 'Cause I talked to her, Dad."

"You *what*?"

44

We heard the tapping of high-heeled shoes on the porch. The doorbell rang, gonging through the house like church bells. *Bong, bong, bong, BONG.*

So that was how Principal Harris met the Watsons, with the four of us cowering in the hall like we thought she'd come to shoot us. She looked very surprised.

For more than half an hour Principal Harris talked with Mom and Dad in the living room. She invited me to join them, but Dad wouldn't allow it. I was sent upstairs with Bumble, and though I tried to listen through the heating vent in the floor, I couldn't hear what they were saying.

After the principal left, my parents kept talking. Mom was the loudest, and some of her words came through the vent. *He can't live like this forever. Put yourself in his place. If he follows the rules, there's no problem; you said so yourself.*

When Dad called for me to come downstairs, I expected him to be angry. But he was *furious*. Standing at the bottom of the stairs, glaring up at me, he looked like a snake. His eyes were little slits, his mouth a thin line. "You have no idea what trouble you've started," he said.

We're bugging out. That was what I thought he would say. But Mom came breezing out of the living room with a big smile on her face.

"You're the one who needs a new suit," she said.

I didn't know how she'd convinced Dad to go along with it, but I was starting school.

Of course there was a catch. Mom would have to drive me there in the morning and drive me back right after school.

"But I can go out again, can't I?" I asked. "I can still stay out until dark. Right?"

Dad shook his head. "You'll have homework. If you go to school, the rules change."

I didn't argue. I was so happy, I didn't care.

AROUND THE LION

I refused to go to school in a suit. But I did let Mom take me to Value Village after dinner and pick out a bunch of clothes for me. Even that was a bit of an adventure. I hardly ever went shopping with my mother, and I'd never gone to Value Village. It was amazing. I'd never seen so much junk in one place.

Mom bought me three shirts and two pairs of pants, a pencil case, and a metal lunch box with pictures of Spider-Man all over it. When she drove me to school on Wednesday morning, I thought I looked pretty cool. But I wasn't sure about the lunch box. "You think kids really use these?" I asked.

"If they don't, they should," said Mom. "They're very practical."

She came into the school to get me registered, and everything was going pretty well until Principal Harris asked for a contact number.

"Why do you need that?" asked Mom.

"In case of emergency," said the principal. "We might have to get hold of you. Or Igor's father."

"I understand," said Mom. She opened her purse, and I watched her sort through the things inside. She found a brochure for Fun and Games and read out the phone number.

Principal Harris gave Mom a funny look and then handed me my schedule. "I'll take you up to room 242 for earth science," she said.

"Should I come along?" asked Mom.

"No!" I told her.

Principal Harris was more tactful. "That won't be necessary," she said.

Classes had already started, and I felt a little nervous as we walked through the empty halls. I wondered: What if Dad was right and the kids laughed at my name? What if nobody talked to me? What if nobody liked me?

"Room 242 will be your homeroom, and your locker's right outside it," said Principal Harris. "But you'll need something to carry your things from class to class. Most of the kids use a backpack."

We came to the stairs and started up to the second floor. The clicking of the principal's shoes echoed back and forth.

"Did you bring your lunch?"

I held up my Spider-Man box.

"Oh, my."

That was the last thing she said until we got to the door of room 242. Then she looked down and asked, "Are you ready?"

I nodded.

"You missed homeroom today, but you'll have it here every morning with Mr. Little. You'll also come back at the end of the day for your last class, which is a free period. So you'll see a lot of Mr. Little. I think you'll like him."

She knocked on the door, waited a moment, and pushed it open. Mr. Little was right there, coming to let us in. Only a couple of inches taller than me, he looked like a rumpled elf in pants too long and a jacket too big. Only the very tips of his fingers poked from his sleeves.

I did like Mr. Little. I liked him right away. But when he stepped aside and I saw thirty kids staring at me from their desks, I felt super hot all of a sudden. In my coat and big boots I must have looked like an explorer straight from the North Pole, carrying his lunch in a Spider-Man box. I tried to hide it behind my back.

Mr. Little put his hand on my shoulder. "Class, this is Igor Watson," he said.

Dad was right. People *did* laugh. They chuckled and snickered, and one kid brayed like a donkey. *Hee-haw.* But above all the laughter one girl called out, "Whoa! Cool name."

I recognized her as the girl on the concrete lion. She sat by the windows, wearing silver jewelry that sparkled in the sunlight. Her face was painted white with makeup, her lips and eyes the deepest black. The lion rider was a Goth.

"You can take that seat in the back," Mr. Little told me. He pointed to an empty desk at the back of the room, beside the boy with the hee-haw laugh.

The room was set up like a theater, with the desks in long rows and an aisle down the middle. Every head turned to watch me as I jingled along in my boots. Hot and sweaty, I slipped into my seat and put my lunch box on the floor beside me.

Mr. Little was talking about the Ice Age. But I was more interested in studying the kids. The boy beside me, the one with the hee-haw laugh, had big teeth and long legs and hands so large that he might have borrowed them from his dad. The Goth girl had silver chains around her neck and tiny crosses dangling from her ears. When she reached up to touch her hair, I saw that her fingernails were painted black, and they slid down her neck like shimmering beetles.

"As the glaciers retreated, they left behind huge boulders they had carried along," said Mr. Little. "You can see some of them down by the river. Anyone know what they're called?"

I knew the answer. But I didn't want to draw attention to myself by holding up my hand.

"Come on. Anybody?" asked Mr. Little.

He gave up and wrote the word on the blackboard. "Erratics," he said. "Two hundred years ago people thought the devil had dropped them from the sky. Erratics were out of place. Bizarre and inexplicable."

He might have been describing me, something snatched from one place and dumped in another where it didn't belong. That first day lasted forever. I wandered from class to class without talking to anybody, and nobody talked to me. At noon, I ate my lunch alone, then shoved my Spider-Man box into a garbage can. When the buzzer rang at the end of the day, Room 242 emptied in an instant. I was left behind like a big, dumb rock.

I walked out the front door to see fresh snow covering the ground. The Goth was up on the lion's back, wearing her long black coat and combat boots. A group of kids stood below her. From the top of the steps, I heard them talking.

"Maybe he's mute," said a girl with red hair.

Somebody asked, "Don't you love the lunch box?" and everyone laughed, like it was the most hilarious thing in the world.

"Did you see his *clothes*?" asked another girl. "They're so *shiny*!"

The Goth said, "They're old-man clothes."

I wanted to slip back into the school and leave by a different door. But it was too late for that. I went down the steps and past the kids like I didn't even know they were there.

"What a loser," someone said.

I felt myself blush. Then the hee-haw kid started chanting, and others joined in, hooting like foghorns. "Eeeeeeegor. Eeeeeeeegor!"

Out on the street stood a convoy of minivans. Beside the jelly bean car, my mom stood waving.

Don't do that! I told her under my breath. As I came closer she walked around the front of the car like she wanted to hug me or kiss me. Afraid the kids were watching, I dodged around her and climbed into the van through the sliding door.

Bumble screamed hello from her car seat. She held Hideous George toward me so I could shake his little hand. In the front, Mom buckled herself slowly into her seat. "Where's your lunch box?" she asked.

"I lost it," I said.

"Oh, what a shame. We'll have to replace that for you."

"No, Mom," I said. "It's okay."

"But—"

"I don't need another one."

"Well, whatever you think." She put on her turn signal and pulled out from the curb. When we were safely away from the school I climbed into the passenger's seat. Mom looked over and asked, "So how was your first day?"

"Terrible!" I said.

"Why?" she asked. "What was so terrible?"

"Everything!" I said. "Dad was right. I don't fit in."

"Give it time," said Mom. "Maybe tomorrow—"

"I don't know if I'm going back," I said.

She risked a sideways glance at me, looking away from the road for a tenth of a second. "So you want to quit?" she asked. "Already?"

"Maybe."

I slouched in my seat and put my feet on the dashboard. Dad would have swatted them down, but Mom just looked mildly annoyed.

Behind us Bumble shouted again. "Mom, George is hungry. He wants to stop and get candy!"

"Well, he's going to be a disappointed little monkey," said Mom. "He doesn't want to rot his teeth, does he?"

"He doesn't have any teeth!" yelled Bumble.

"And maybe that's why."

Bumble laughed.

We drove along Jefferson, past Fun and Games. But Dad wasn't out on the sidewalk.

"Where's the clown?" I asked.

"If you mean your father, he probably got off early and went home," said Mom.

But he wasn't there either. No one except Mom and Bumble had walked on the fresh snow.

"That's funny," said Mom.

She sounded more curious than concerned. I figured Dad would show up before long, and Bumble didn't seem to care at all. "Do you want to build a snowman, Igor?" she asked.

"Sure," I said. "Okay, Mom?"

"As long as you don't build it anywhere near the river," she told me. "And change out of those clothes first. You'll ruin them."

"Good," I said.

"Now what's that supposed to mean?"

"They're old man's clothes," I told her. "I hate them."

"What, just because they're polyester? Honey, they're not 'old man's clothes. Don't worry about what people think."

Mom got Bumble out of the car, then knelt in the snow to fasten her little boots. I had a funny feeling she would turn around when she'd finished and tighten my buckles. But she went into the house to wait for Dad, and Bumble and I walked down to the backyard. In the gloomy gray shadow of the apartment buildings next door, we began to build our snowman.

We started with a handful of snow and rolled it up and down the yard. It was more than two feet high when Bumble stopped to make an angel. She fell backward into the snow and started fanning her arms and legs. I sat on the snowman's partly built body, looking off toward the river.

In the forest on the other side, a little flurry of snowflakes fell from a tree. I saw branches bending and a larger clump of snow falling loose. And then a half-hidden face appeared in the shadows of the bushes.

It was an awful shock. I stood up and motioned to Bumble. "Let's go inside."

"Why?" she asked.

I didn't want to scare her. I said, "I'm getting cold."

"But I want to finish the snowman."

"We can finish it tomorrow."

I reached down to grab on to her snowsuit. But Bumble cried, "No!" She rolled onto her side and curled up like a pill bug. "I want to do it now."

The man was moving behind the bushes, crawling toward the river. "Bumble, come on," I said, and tried to pull her up.

She started crying. She just would not move.

This was the moment I'd been warned about for years, and I felt like I was stuck in one of my terrible dreams, scared to look back, unable to run. I shouted, "Mom!"

Someone must have heard me in their apartment high above us. A sliding door banged open. A face appeared at a railing. Mom came dashing out onto the back porch. "Igor, what's wrong?" she cried.

Bumble wailed as I pulled her along by the sleeve. She kicked her little feet as she slid through the snow. I was so scared that I almost left her there. But I whirled around to pick her up, and in that moment I saw the man rising to his feet. Snow fell away from his shoulders and his arms.

"Mom!" I clutched Bumble's collar and dragged her through the snow. Mom was running down the steps to help me.

The man's voice carried over the river. "It's all right. It's me."

I stopped and looked toward him. I saw Dad waving from the edge of the forest.

"It's just me," he said.

He came out of the bushes in his clown pants, a jacket on top. He plowed through the snow to the riverbank, then waggled his arms and shouted, "It's okay!"

It took Dad nearly half an hour to walk back to the house, but Mom was *still* furious. "What on earth were you doing over there?" she asked.

"Scouting," he said, like it was the most reasonable thing in the world. "I wanted to see what someone would see from there."

"So you hid in the forest to frighten your children?" asked Mom.

"I'm only trying to keep them safe," he said.

THE BOOKS

I dreaded going to school the next day. I kept remembering the kids laughing at me, the taunting cry behind my back. *Eeeeeeegor. Eeeeeeeegor.* How could I go through that again?

My parents watched me fiddle with my breakfast, and it wasn't hard for them to guess what I was thinking. "You know, son, you don't have to go back," Dad told me. "You can stay here and do your homeschooling."

"I bet you'd like that," I said.

He only sighed. But Mom told me, "We want what you want."

That was no help. "I don't *know* what I want," I said.

Dad went upstairs to get ready for work. With Bumble still asleep, only Mom and I were left in the kitchen.

"I'm going to tell you a story," she said.

"Oh, boy. It's my lucky day."

She pulled out a chair and sat down beside me. "When I was little girl, my father made me take piano lessons," she said. "I hated him for that."

"Oh, Mom." I didn't care about her stupid piano lessons.

"Now just listen," she said. "I kicked and I screamed. I made such a fuss that my father gave up after only two weeks. 'You don't want to go, that's fine with me,' he said. So I quit. And you know what? I've regretted it ever since. I'm sorry I never learned to play the piano."

It was a dumb story, maybe not even true. But it made me decide that I *did* want to go to school. Because I *didn't* want to sit at home with my mom anymore. When Dad came back into the kitchen, he was wearing his clown suit. As he adjusted his huge bow tie, he asked, "So what's the verdict?"

I said, "I'll go to school."

"That's great," said Mom, smiling at me.

Dad wasn't so happy, but he didn't argue. "Well, if you're sure about this, you might as well let your mother drive you there right now."

I didn't want to be seen driving up with my mom in the bright green minivan. I said, "I'd rather walk."

"You'll do no such thing," said Dad. "We made a deal. Your mother will drive you."

"I walked there before," I said.

"I know that," said Dad. "And you won't do it again. If you don't want your mother to drive you, I'll get the keys and—"

"No!" I said. The very last thing I wanted was to be driven to school by a clown in a minivan.

So I went with my mom, and because I didn't have a backpack yet, I carried my things in a grocery bag.

I was more than half an hour early, the first kid in room 242. As Mr. Little wrote things on the blackboard, I took my seat and started fiddling with my pen. The other kids arrived in little groups, laughing and talking all around me.

"Take your seats, please," said Mr. Little.

The hee-haw boy tumbled into his chair next to mine like he'd fallen from an airplane. Soon only one kid was left standing. Right beside me, he gripped the corner of my desk and shook it.

"You're in my place," he said.

He had not been at school the day before, or I would have noticed him for sure. He had a scrunched-up face with lumpy little ears, his hair too long on one side, too short on the other. I guessed his mother was his barber.

"Get out!" The boy jiggled my desk again. He shoved my books aside and plonked down his backpack. "Move!" he told me.

Mr. Little sighed. "Angelo, what's the problem?"

"This dork's in my place," said the boy.

"Then sit somewhere else." Mr. Little pointed to an empty desk in the middle of the room, on the aisle that split the class. "That place is empty."

"I don't want to sit there," said Angelo, as whiny as a three-year-old.

"Feel free to leave, Mr. Bonito."

With a scowl, Angelo grabbed his backpack. As he turned away, it banged against my head, not by accident.

The hee-haw boy leaned closer and whispered, "He'll get you for that."

I was aware of Angelo Bonito all through that morning, as we moved from class to class. Whenever I saw him, he was taking up an awful lot of space, always talking loudly. Of all the kids I wouldn't want to be mad at me, Angelo Bonito would be top of the list.

Right after lunch, our math teacher handed out a pop quiz and told us to bring them up to her desk as we finished.

I had to pass Angelo on the way there, and then again on the way back, and at that moment he reached out his hand to stop me. He pointed at the floor.

His books lay scattered next to his desk.

"Pick them up," he told me.

"Why?"

"You knocked them down. Pick 'em up."

I knew I hadn't knocked down his books, and I wasn't going to get onto my knees and pick them up just to give him a laugh. I stepped right over them. A few minutes later I watched Angelo bend down to collect them. I could see a band of his underwear peeking up above the seat of his pants. There was something about the way he had to stretch and grope that made me feel sorry for him. But as soon as the teacher turned away, Angelo turned to me. He pointed a finger like a stabbing knife. "I'm going to kill you," he mouthed.

The hee-haw boy nodded at me. "He will," he whispered. "He'll kill you."

Through the rest of that day I couldn't think of anything except Angelo and his stupid books and what would happen as soon as school ended. I imagined myself lying in different arrangements under the concrete lion, with a chalk outline drawn around my body.

In the final period, back in Mr. Little's room, the clock at the front counted down my last minutes. The long finger of the second hand moved in tiny leaps until the buzzer rang to end the day.

I got up and joined the rush for the door. Like water

through a funnel, it swept me out into the hall and down to my locker. I saw Angelo's goofy face and his weird haircut bobbing past.

I took out my coat and put it on. All around me, the metal doors of the lockers were clanging shut, kids were shouting, and that river of people was surging along.

I could have thrown myself into it and tried to escape in the flood. But Angelo was a little bit downstream, standing by his open locker. The hee-haw kid was there beside him, the two of them watching me, waiting for me to go floating past.

There was no way I was going to do that. I went back to the room and sat at my desk. I emptied my grocery bag and filled it again, as slowly as I possibly could. Each pencil, each pen, each piece of paper, I placed carefully inside.

There were a few stragglers still leaving, and the noise in the hall was beginning to fade. I imagined that Angelo had gone outside with everyone else and was waiting for me by the concrete lions like a spider in its web.

Well, he'll have a long wait, I thought. I decided to sneak out of the school through a back door. If I could find one.

I was about to put that plan into action when Angelo and the hee-haw boy strolled into the room again.

Mr. Little looked up but didn't say anything. He couldn't leave until the room was empty.

I started taking stuff out of my bag all over again, like I'd suddenly remembered I had to make more notes. The boys wandered across the room to look at Mr. Little's displays of rocks and fossils and dead insects.

It was probably the first time *any* kid had stayed late to look at those things, and Mr. Little must have been amazed. He closed his books and leaned back in his chair.

"Interested in butterflies, Trevis?" he asked.

"Who isn't?" said the hee-haw boy.

Mr. Little walked over and stood between them. He was about the same height as Angelo and at least a foot shorter than Trevis.

"Look at this." He pointed into one of the cases. "That's an owl butterfly, that brownish one," he said. "See how those spots on its wings mimic the eyes of an owl? Here, look closely."

The boys bent down, their hands on the sides of the wooden box.

I knew they didn't care about butterflies, and it made me feel sad to see Mr. Little so enthusiastic. Then I started wondering if he knew exactly what was going on and only wanted to give me a chance to escape.

I shoved my things back in my bag, bent down, and tightened the buckles on my boots. Quiet as a ninja, I left the room. In the hall I started running. I turned right, then left, then left again, past a janitor with a cart full of garbage bags, a teacher who shouted at me to "Walk, don't run!" I bounded down a flight of stairs, bashed open a metal door, and stumbled out onto the playground. Across the field, over the snow, I went at a dead run. Only when I reached the street did I stop to catch my breath. Then, like a spy on the loose, I dashed from tree to tree and made my way to the front of the school.

The green jelly bean was the only car left. Mom was standing beside it, shielding her eyes from the sun as she looked around the school yard.

"Oh, thank goodness," she said when I ran up beside her. "I was getting scared."

Well, so was I. Hot air blasted from the minivan when I threw open the sliding door. Bumble was there, laughing at me as I dove inside. "Let's go," I said.

"Don't you want to sit up front?" asked Mom.

"It's nice back here."

Mom pushed hard on the sliding door. It closed with a whoosh and a thump that rocked the whole van. I lifted my head and peeked over the seats. Out through the school's front door came Angelo and Trevis.

As they started down the steps, Mom got into the driver's seat. She yanked on her seat belt, hauling it over her shoulder as they walked toward the street.

"Let's go," I said again.

"All right!" In a huff she put the car into drive, turned on the windshield wipers for no reason on earth, and pulled slowly from the curb.

We went right past Angelo and Trevis. I could see Angelo's gnarled little ears, as pink as Bumble's coat. He turned to look right at me, like he somehow felt me watching him.

There was no way he could see through the tinted windows. But I didn't move until Mom rounded the corner at the next block. When I raised my head, I saw her watching me in the rearview mirror.

"Do you know those boys?" she asked.

"Sort of."

"Are you in some kind of trouble?"

I wanted to tell her yes, I was in big trouble. Then she could talk to Principal Harris, and someone would tell Angelo to leave me alone. But I knew that wouldn't work. It would only make him angry. So I shook my head and said, "No, Mom."

I was doomed.

That night was terrible. I felt like a guy on death row, hoping for a last-minute pardon. I kept seeing Angelo turning around to point at me. *I'm going to kill you.* I kept hearing Trevis whispering, *He'll get you for that.* Over and over and over, I asked myself, *Why didn't you pick up the STUPID BOOKS???*

At dawn I was still tossing in my bed, looking every minute through the crack in the curtains, hoping to see a sudden, terrible blizzard that would close the school. But that never came, and I knew I couldn't run away from Angelo every day for the rest of my life. There was no choice. I had to go to school and let him kill me.

A HANDFUL OF SNOW

I thought my pardon had arrived.

Again the first kid into the classroom, I watched the others come through the door. I expected Angelo and Trevis to appear at any moment. But when the first bell rang they were the only two who hadn't arrived.

Mr. Little walked over and gave the door a push to swing it shut. But it crashed open again, banging against the wall. In walked Angelo and Travis.

"Glad you could join us, gentlemen," said Mr. Little.

That was a horrible day. I just wanted to get it all over with, and I wouldn't have believed that hours could pass so slowly. When the buzzer rang to end the day, I put my things in my grocery bag, got my coat from my locker, and started walking toward the front door like nothing was wrong. Right away, Trevis was at my side. Another boy fell in behind me. Then Angelo stepped in front, and they herded me down the hall.

Mr. Little watched us from the doorway. "Everything all right, boys?"

"Yes," said Trevis.

"Igor?"

"It's okay," I said.

I could see he was suspicious. If I'd told him I needed help, he would have helped me. But I didn't want to rely on him like Dad relied on the Protectors. I had to do this alone. Corralled by the boys, I was steered down the stairs and out the back door.

It was cold there, on the shadowed side of the building. Under its fresh surface, the snow was old and crunchy. Angelo led us past the gym, to the loneliest part of the playground where teachers never went and the snow was thickest. Suddenly, he whirled around and grabbed my coat. He drove me backward, slamming me against the wall. I dropped my paper bag. The others held my arms and pinned me there, one on each side.

Angelo reached down to grab something. With my head pressed against the cold brick, I couldn't see what it was. But strangely, I didn't care. I didn't shout or blubber or struggle to get away. I just stood there and let Angelo do whatever he meant to do. I saw his hand sweep up again, and in his fist was—

Snow.

He had a handful of snow, and he squashed it into my mouth and my eyes. He forced it between my lips, against my teeth; he pushed it up my nose.

I started laughing. After all the terrible things I'd imagined, the hours of worry and fear, all he did was rub snow in my face.

"Why are you laughing?" he said.

"I don't know," I told him. I tried to stop but couldn't.

Maybe Angelo was only getting started. Maybe he really *was* planning the things I'd imagined—or worse—and to him

I seemed crazy and fearless. Laughing in the face of death. He let the snow fall to the ground and backed away.

"Come on, let's go," he said to his friends. They went slouching across the playground, kicking at the snow. I picked up my bag and went home.

After that day, Angelo never bothered me again. We weren't friends or anything, or not right away. It was more like we'd become invisible to each other. He didn't threaten me, didn't intimidate me, didn't try to kick me out of my place in the classroom. His desk became mine.

THE OUTSIDERS

I got Mom to buy me a backpack, but I wouldn't let her pick it out. I was afraid she'd choose something orange or pink, with unicorns leaping over rainbows.

The one I chose was a nice bland color, but I scuffed it up a bit so it wouldn't look too new. I loved my backpack, and I carried it slung over one shoulder with the straps dangling down, just like the cool kids did.

Every morning I looked forward to going to school, and the days passed quickly. Soon it was March and winter was ending. Out on the river, huge cracks appeared in the ice. Snow turned to slush and melted away. But the apartment-shaded lawn of the yellow house remained a gray island of winter, deep with snow.

In language arts, our teacher split the class into groups to study *The Call of the Wild*. I couldn't figure out why she put me with Angelo and Trevis and the Goth, but every Wednesday afternoon we pushed our desks into a clump in the corner and got to work. Each group had to give a presentation, and we chose "Wolves of the Yukon."

The Goth was named Zoe, and in our group she was the smartest by far. She was our researcher.

Angelo was the artist. If *I* drew a wolf it looked like a guinea pig, but Angelo's seemed nearly alive. He made the hair thick and layered, so real I wanted to touch it. But if anybody told Angelo he was good at drawing he got mad. He wanted people to think he was tough and mean. In that way, he and Zoe were the same, afraid to let anybody see what they were really like inside.

Trevis was our speaker, the one who'd have to stand up and give our presentation. He wasn't a great speaker, but he didn't mind making a fool of himself.

That first day, I didn't have a job. I didn't even open my mouth. Then Zoe shoved a notebook in front of me and slammed a pen on top.

I looked at her, but all I could see was a little crucifix pinned through her nose. It sparkled in the sun, dazzling me.

"You're the scribe," she said. "Start scribing."

Only Zoe would have used that word. Trevis burst out laughing. "What's a *scribe*?" he said in his hooting voice.

"A writer, you moron," said Zoe.

She passed me all the notes she'd made about wolves. She practically told me what to write, then went back to her research.

I saw her bent over the book with her shiny hair touching the edge of her desk. I saw Angelo drawing bloodstained wolf teeth, the tip of his tongue poking out between his lips, and Trevis sprawled in his chair doing nothing, and I began to see why our language arts teacher had made us a group. We were the outsiders, belonging together because we didn't belong with anyone else. In a supermarket, we would have been the dented cans put aside on a separate shelf.

In a way, that made me a loser. But I didn't care. For the first time in my life I was part of a group. Bit by bit, without even trying, I was becoming part of the freak show known as middle school.

Already it had become my whole life. If I wasn't in school I was thinking about school, remembering things Angelo had said, and Trevis's stupid jokes, and the way Zoe clomped along in her big boots. I spent ages trying to figure her out. Why did she dress like a corpse in a coffin, with her face painted white and her eyelids black? Why did she love shiny metal jewelry so much? I didn't want to hurt her feelings by asking her about it, so I just kept staring. Zoe would have called it *ogling*.

She didn't mind. It was like Zoe *wanted* people to stare at her and wonder what she was all about. They could hate her or like her, and she couldn't care less. But she sure wanted people to notice her.

The next Wednesday, at the end of our study group, we started pushing our desks back into their tidy rows. Zoe turned around to push hers with her butt, and I ogled her big clunky army boots, her little black skirt, her stockings that looked like ripped-up fishing nets.

She stared right back. I saw her eyes traveling up from the floor, noting my shoes, my pants, my shirt. When they reached my face she said, "Why do you dress so weird?"

Well, *she* was a fine one to talk. Had she ever heard of a mirror? Maybe she didn't cast a reflection.

"It's like you raid your dad's closet," she said. "Do you dress in the dark?"

I didn't know what to say. I just stood there, kind of shocked.

"You got any money?" she asked.

I nodded.

"How much?"

I didn't want to tell her.

"Come on," she said. "You think I'm going to rob you?"

"A hundred dollars."

She didn't seem at all surprised. "Well, that *might* be enough."

"For what?"

Zoe smiled. "Meet me after school."

I didn't know what she had in mind, and I didn't have a chance to ask until school was over. At the end of free period, I followed her out of room 242.

"What are we going to do?" I asked.

"You'll see."

"You know, I'm not allowed to spend my money," I said, "if that's what you're thinking."

"Then why do you have it?" she asked.

What would she say if I told her the truth? *I keep it in my sock in case the Lizard Man shows up.* My hundred-dollar bill was supposed to pay for a taxi ride or a motel room or anything I needed. Written on one side was a phone number that would bring help right away, and it was *not* 911.

Our lockers were close together. Zoe kept talking as she opened hers and put away her books. "Well?" she said. "If you can't spend it, why do you have it?"

"I dunno."

"You say that all the time. 'I dunno; I dunno.' " She reached behind her neck and pulled her hair up over the collar of her coat. She let it fall around her shoulders, black and stiff and shiny. Her jewelry glittered. "Igor, you're weird."

We went down the stairs and out the front door.

I should have told her my mother was waiting. I should have said I wasn't allowed to go wandering around after school. But I didn't. I just followed Zoe out through the gate and north toward Jefferson Street.

Out of the corner of my eye, I saw the green minivan. I thought I saw my mother standing beside it, watching me, but I didn't look hard enough to be sure. I wondered what I would do if she pulled up beside me and told me, "Get in." But that didn't happen. I'd broken one of Dad's rules, and a little while later I broke another one.

Zoe crossed Jefferson, and I followed her. It was only to the other side, so I told myself it didn't really matter. I was not going *past* Jefferson Street. We walked west toward the river, past stores and coffee shops. I thought everyone was staring at us, until I realized they were seeing only Zoe. I might have been invisible, a silent gray shadow.

"How did you get the name Igor?" she asked.

I couldn't tell her *that* story either. I mumbled, "I dunno."

"You know who Igor is?"

"Yeah, from *Frankenstein*."

"From *Dracula*, dummy. Igor's a servant in Dracula's castle in Transylvania. He eats bugs."

"I didn't know that."

"He's a Gypsy."

An old lady driving a silver car gaped at us through her

windshield. She turned on the wipers, squirting water on the glass.

"So why did you pick that name?" asked Zoe.

"Who says I did?"

"Oh, come on," she said. "Nobody names their kid Igor. So you must have picked it yourself."

"Did you pick the name Zoe?" I asked.

"Yes," she said, surprising me. "It's from a game I used to play. *Relentless.*"

"Never heard of it."

"Why would you? It's a stupid game. This girl called Zoe escapes from an asylum."

She strode along beside me with her hands in her pockets. I thought of my mother standing beside the minivan.

"I think people should change names every year," said Zoe. "Like on January first you pick a new one." She glanced at me sideways. "How long have you been Igor?"

"Always," I said.

"Oh, come on."

She knew I was lying, but I stuck to my story. If I admitted to inventing my name she'd ask what name I'd had before, and we'd go around and around till she knew the truth. I couldn't let that happen. Like Dad always said, Zoe could know someone who knew someone else who knew the Lizard Man.

We passed a theater on a corner. A faint crackling from its neon sign made me look up, and I saw the tubes pulsing with a dim red glow, spelling out the name of the theater. The Bijou.

"Look," said Zoe. She was pointing at something up ahead. "See that crazy old clown?"

She meant my dad. He was two or three blocks away, on the other side of the street, pacing the sidewalk in his stupid clown clothes. His baggy pants swung around him as he turned this way and that way, holding out pamphlets that no one even looked at.

"He's always there with those dumb brochures," said Zoe. "I heard he works for Homeland Security or something. He's on a stakeout."

Of course I didn't let on that the "crazy old clown" was my dad. I stepped up close beside Zoe and made her my bodyguard. Shielded by her black coat, I walked past a store with shiny windows. Our reflections zoomed across the glass, a Goth in startling black and white, a boy in a plain blue coat. My dad didn't even glance toward me as we reached the corner of Dead End Road and turned to the right.

A FRIEND OF FANNY'S

I stopped just around the corner, as soon as we were safely out of sight. Zoe was taking me exactly where Dad had told me not to go, straight up the street I'd been tempted to explore on my very first day. When she realized I wasn't beside her anymore, she turned and looked back.

"You coming?" she asked. "It's just up here."

"What?"

"The army store."

That sounded cool. I imagined myself buying camouflage clothes and ammo belts, combat boots like Zoe's. I *had* to go to a place like that, so I tagged along, up a block and left again, staying close to the river.

Zoe took me to a little wooden building that had once been a church. There was still a stained-glass window high on the wall, above a painted sign. Zoe's "army store" was the Salvation Army.

A little bell rang as we went in. Behind the cash register, on a tall stool, a lady sat reading a romance novel.

"Hi, Mom," said Zoe.

The woman was a lot older than my mom and didn't look at all like Zoe. She had silvery hair, bright lipstick, and reading glasses with a gold chain that looped down her neck. She lifted them from her nose and squinted underneath. "Well, hello," she said. "This is a nice surprise. And who's your friend?"

"There's no time to talk," said Zoe. "It's an emergency."

The woman went back to her reading, and Zoe went shopping. For half an hour she kept pulling clothes from racks and holding them against me to see how they looked. She sometimes had two or three in each hand, shoving coat hangers back and forth along the racks. Once in a while she said, "Try this one on," and I went into a little booth with a curtain for a door. It didn't go nearly to the floor, and I had to hold it closed with one hand as Zoe hovered outside.

She picked out five T-shirts, a pair of chinos, and a pair of jeans. When I stood head to foot in new clothes she hauled me over to a full-length mirror. "What do you think?" she asked.

I saw a stranger staring back at me, the sort of kid I'd always *wanted* to look like. I turned back and forth to admire myself. "Now you look normal," said Zoe.

She grabbed my old clothes from the changing room floor and piled them on the counter. "Can we leave these here?" she asked. "Maybe someone will want them for Halloween."

Her mother rang everything up on the register, stuffed the clothes into a bag, and told me, "That's seventeen dollars."

She stared at me, waiting. So did Zoe. There was nothing I could do but bend down and take off my shoe, and then my sock. I shook out the hundred-dollar bill and began to unfold the creases.

Nobody said that was strange. Nobody asked why a kid would walk around with money in his sock. But as soon as Zoe's mom saw the picture of Franklin on the bill she freaked out.

"Who do you think I am? Mrs. Rockefeller?" she asked. "Don't you have anything smaller?"

"No," I told her.

"Try your other sock," said Zoe.

Her mother opened the till and sorted through the money inside. Zoe nudged me. "What's that phone number?" she asked, pointing at my hundred-dollar bill. I pretended like I had no idea.

There wasn't much money in the till. "I'll tell you what," said Zoe's mom. "It's my treat."

"Thanks," I said, "but I can't—"

"Nonsense." She pushed my money toward me. "You're a friend of Fanny's, and that's good enough for me."

Fanny? I would have laughed out loud, except that I felt a warm glow running through me. *A friend of Fanny's*—I loved the sound of that. I had never been a friend of anybody's.

I squashed my hundred-dollar bill into my pocket and led Zoe to the door. Outside, on the sidewalk, she put her hands on my arms and held me tightly. "Igor," she said. "Please don't ever call me Fanny."

"Okay," I said. "I won't."

"And don't tell anybody else. Ever."

I looked right into her eyes. I had never done that with anyone other than Mom and Dad and Bumble, and it felt strange. I could see Zoe's pupils twitching back and forth. There were tiny cracks in her black makeup.

"Promise me, Igor," she said. "Kids can be mean."

Well, I knew all about *that*. But it surprised me that Zoe would even worry about it. Maybe under those torn clothes, behind the makeup and the silver crosses, there was a girl who actually did care what people thought of her. I said, "I'll never tell anybody."

With a smile she tightened her fingers, squeezing my arms. "Thanks, Igor."

Suddenly she was Zoe again, stepping back, turning so fast that her coat billowed around her. She shoved her hands in her pockets and asked, "You want to go to Deadman's Castle?"

"There's a castle?" I said.

"No, it's just a place. On the hill across the river." She motioned with her hand, spreading her coat like bat wings. "Come on, I'll show you."

It was very tempting to go with her. But if I crossed the river I'd never get home before dark, and I'd break all Dad's rules before I got home. I wondered if my mom was still waiting outside the school. "I can't," I said. "I have to go home."

"Why?"

" 'Cause I do."

With a shrug she turned and walked away. Her combat boots thunked on the sidewalk, her coat swished against her legs. I shouted after her, "See you tomorrow."

Zoe didn't look back.

MR. MORON'S HAT

At the yellow house, I walked past the jelly bean car in the driveway. In my mind I was trying to come up with excuses to tell Mom and Dad. *I got stuck in school. Sorry. My teacher kept me late. I had to look at Mr. Little's butterflies.* None of them was very good, and I didn't know how I was going to explain the bag of clothes, or even the ones I was wearing.

They all met me at the door, Mom and Dad and Bumble too. Like always, Bumble was happy to see me, but Dad sent her into the living room. I could hear her favorite DVD playing in there. She was watching *Thomas the Tank Engine,* the world's most obnoxious train.

Mom crossed her arms. She looked angry, but not nearly as angry as Dad.

"Where have you been?" he said. Then he suddenly noticed my new clothes, and he practically shouted, "You went *shopping.*"

"Dad—"

"You didn't spend your lifeline, did you?"

"No," I said.

"Then where did you get the money?"

"I didn't need any," I told him.

"Oh, clothes grow on trees now, do they?" He sounded so sarcastic. "What sort of store gives away clothes?"

"The Salvation Army," I told him. "See, they're old."

I held up the bag, and Dad peered inside it. He lifted a T-shirt with the very tips of his fingers, like he thought it was covered with lice. "So where's the Salvation Army?" he asked.

"Just over—"

"I know where it is!" he snapped. "It's on the other side of Jefferson. You broke the rules."

"But—"

"You also left your mother standing outside the school while you went wandering around with a strange girl."

Mom butted in. "I saw you walking up the street. Why didn't you at least come and tell me where you were going?"

"You wouldn't have let me go!" I said.

"What's that girl's name?" asked Dad.

"Zoe," I said.

"Zoe *what*?"

"I don't know," I told him. I couldn't remember ever hearing her last name.

"If you can't go to school without the breaking the rules," said Dad, "maybe you shouldn't go at all."

I was afraid he was going to tell me next that I couldn't go back to school. But Mom stepped in again.

"Did that girl take you shopping?" she asked. "Is that what happened? She helped you pick out those clothes?"

"Yes," I said. "They're cool, see?"

I tried to move like a model, swinging out my hips as I spread my arms. But Dad wasn't impressed.

"Clothes don't make the man," he said.

But this time he was wrong.

When I went to school the next day I felt like a different kid. Girls who had never said hello told me they liked my clothes. Even Mr. Moran, the gym teacher, noticed. As he passed through the locker room on the way to his office, he held up a thumb and shouted at me in his booming voice. "Lookin' good, Igor!"

I always felt sorry for Mr. Moran. The kids called him Mr. Moron and made fun of him because he couldn't throw a football very far or shoot a three pointer to save his life. But he was nice to me, and I liked him.

That day, it was cold in the locker room. I saw goose bumps on my legs as I took off my new clothes and put on my stuff for gym. We all had to wear white socks; that was the rule. The kids thought I was strange because I pulled mine right over the ones I was wearing. But they had gotten tired of joking about it, and no one even mentioned it that afternoon.

Mr. Moran came out of his office. The sin bin, he called it, because he made kids sit in there when they were bad. He was wearing what he always wore, a gray sweat suit with a whistle hanging around his neck. He used both hands to put on his red baseball cap, one at the back, one tugging down on the brim.

Trevis asked, "Are we going to the gym or out to the field, Mr. Moran?"

"Look at the hat, Trevis!" Mr. Moran pointed at himself,

jabbing his finger like he was poking his eye. "I wear the hat, we go outside."

Some of the kids laughed. It was an old joke to ask him that question, because he always gave the same answer, but poor Mr. Moran never seemed to catch on.

We went out and played soccer, though the day was pretty cold and the ball felt half frozen. I kept to the edges of the field until Mr. Moran blew his whistle and called me over.

"You're hangin' back, Igor," he said. "You're not goin' after the ball. What's the matter, afraid of gettin' hurt?"

"Yes," I said. I wasn't stupid.

"Look, Igor, it isn't goin' to kill you," said Mr. Moran. "You get hit, so what?"

"It hurts," I told him. Half the kids had huge pink circles on their skin. We might have been playing soccer with a bowling ball.

"Let me tell you somethin', Igor." Mr. Moran lifted his red cap and brushed back his hair. "The way a guy plays ball, that's how he lives his life. Stay out and stay safe, or go in and take your shots."

I nodded like I understood.

"Winners don't stay safe, Igor. Up to you."

He sent me back into the game. I ran right for the ball, into the crowd of kids, and I got smacked in the thigh two minutes later. The ball left a mark like a tomato. But I scored a goal. It was the first goal I'd ever scored and it won the game, and every kid on my team crowded around to clap me

on the back. They started chanting their old chant—*Ee-gor!*
Ee-gor!—but now in a friendly way that made me feel like a
hero. I held my hands high above my head and jogged slowly
across the field.

Ee-gor! Ee-gor!

It was, without a doubt, the greatest moment of my life.

THE SITTER

Mom and Dad never went out together. One always stayed home to stand guard. So when Parents' Night came along later in March and they both wanted to go, it seemed like a fight might break out.

"I think I'd better see what that school's all about," said Dad over dinner. "I'd like to meet your teachers."

"So would I," said Mom.

Then they sat there and stared at each other.

It was still a few days before Parents' Night, but I didn't think that would give them enough time to work it out. I said, "Why don't you both go?"

"We can't," said Dad.

"Why?" I asked. "It's not like it's late at night or anything. You'll be back in an hour. I can look after Bumble."

Mom shrugged. She tipped her head and smiled at Dad. "What do you think?"

"I don't know. We'll see," said Dad.

The next day, to my surprise, they said they were both going to Parents' Night. It was the first time I would be left alone with Bumble, and I looked forward to that. But Bumble dreaded it.

On that Thursday we ate an early dinner. Then Mom went to get dressed up, and Bumble followed her asking, "Why can't I go with you?"

"Because it's only for grown-ups," said Mom. "Don't worry, Bumblebee. We'll be back before you know it."

It was awful to see how desperately my sister clung to Mom. They had barely been out of each other's sight for all of Bumble's life. I had to go to the top of the stairs and peel her fingers from Mom's ankle, one by one, like I was tearing a starfish from a rock. "Come on, let's go downstairs," I said. "What do you want to do?"

I thought we'd end up watching one of her DVDs. But Bumble said, "Let's play Uncle Wiggily."

I couldn't help groaning. I hated that stupid game. Whenever we saw a dead rabbit beside the road I told Bumble, "Look, there's Uncle Wiggily." But then I remembered.

"We don't have that game anymore," I said. "We left it behind in the old house."

Bumble looked sad for a moment, then happy again. "So let's pretend!"

If there's anything worse than playing Uncle Wiggily, it's pretending to play Uncle Wiggily. But that was what we did. As Mom and Dad got ready for Parents' Night, I sat on the living room floor with my little sister and Hideous George, playing a board game that didn't exist. We picked imaginary cards from an imaginary pile and walked our fingers along the floor to Dr. Possum's house.

At six o'clock Mom appeared in the doorway. Her feet were bare, her toenails painted red. She was holding a pair of shoes.

"You look pretty, Mom," said Bumble.

"Oh, thank you." Mom had never smiled so nicely. She

leaned against the doorjamb and pulled on one of her shoes. "We'll be leaving in a few minutes, Igor."

"Great, Mom," I said.

"As soon as your sitter gets here."

No one had mentioned that. "My *sitter*?" I said.

"Her name's Amy," said Mom. "She lives in the big apartment building next door."

"Does Dad know about her?"

"Of course. He interviewed her."

"Did he fingerprint her?"

"Don't be silly."

I stood up and faced my mother. Bumble shrieked at me, "You're standing on Uncle Wiggily!" but I ignored her. I said, "Mom, I'll be thirteen this year. I can look after Bumble by myself."

"I'm sure you can," said Mom. "But we're not leaving you alone, and that's the end of it."

"Why?"

"You know very well why," she said. "Someone has to make sure you're safe."

"So call the army," I told her.

"Oh, don't be dramatic."

Bumble was watching. In one hand she held an imaginary card, waiting to ask me to read it. Her little fingers were actually pinching something that only she could see.

"I would love to go out and not have to worry," said Mom. "But I can't. Not with that lunatic around."

"You mean Dad?"

Her mouth fell open. "How dare you say that?" she said.

The doorbell rang. Bumble cast away her invisible card and leapt up with a shout. "I'll get it!"

She raced to the door like she always did, forgetting that she couldn't reach the lock. Mom was busy with her shoes, so I went to help Bumble. But Dad came thundering down the stairs with his tie undone, anxious to see for himself who was out there. No one got in without being vetted.

Bumble crouched down and peeked through the letter slot. Dad, towering above her, put his eye to the peephole, and the two of them stared out like U-boat captains at their periscopes.

"Okay," said Dad. "She's clear." He went back upstairs, leaving me and Bumble to let Amy in. I turned the dead bolt and flicked the chain from its catch, and Bumble pushed me out of the way. She loved to open the door. She gripped the knob with both hands and pulled it open.

There stood Amy, six feet tall and thinner than a skeleton, with green hair even shorter than Dad's. In faded jeans, her skinny legs looked like swimming noodles.

Bumble clasped her hands behind her back, looked way up, and said, "Hi! I'm Bumble."

"Well, hi to you too." Amy had a canvas bag slung over her shoulder, her fingers tucked under the strap. She looked at me and asked, like I was eight years old, "And what's *your* name?"

"Igor."

Amy laughed. She asked, "Is your master at home?"

I didn't even answer. Mom stepped out of the living room and gawked at Amy's hair. At the same time, Dad came down the stairs to give Amy what he must have thought were the normal rules for babysitters: "Keep the curtains shut. Lock the door and don't open it for anyone unless you hear our special knock." He rapped it out on the wall with his knuckles: *tap-tap-tap, tap-tap-tap.* "Got it?"

"Yes," said Amy. And then, both smiling, Mom and Dad went out the door.

Bumble didn't mind them leaving if Amy was there. She reached up and took her hand. "We're playing Uncle Wiggily," she said.

"Oh, good." Amy let herself be pulled into the living room. She looked down at Hideous George sitting in the middle of the floor and asked, "Where's the game?"

"You have to pretend."

That was Amy's introduction to the wonderful world of the Watsons. I felt embarrassed. "Maybe we should watch a movie," she said.

"Okay," said Bumble. "Do you like *My Little Pony*?"

"Love it."

I would have liked to take My Little Pony out behind the barn and shoot him. But I sat down to watch because there wasn't anything else to do. Amy stretched out on the sofa.

"Does everyone who comes over have to give a secret knock?" she asked.

"Nobody comes over," I said.

Bumble put in the DVD of *My Little Pony* and sat on the floor with her grumpy. She'd seen the movie at least a thousand times, and she kept looking up to tell us everything that was going to happen a minute before it did.

Amy ignored her. "Your dad has a lot of rules," she said. "He's just being protective," I told her.

For five minutes she lay there on the sofa and stared around the room. Then she said, "You don't have any photographs."

"What do you mean?" I asked.

"On the *walls*," she said, like I was stupid. "There's no *stuff* in this house. It's like you don't really live here. There's no knickknacks. No souvenirs. *Everyone* has souvenirs."

"Oh, you've been to everyone's house?" I asked.

Amy didn't recognize sarcasm. She kept gazing at the empty walls, the empty shelves, the empty tabletops. "There's no wedding pictures. No baby pictures," she said. "Didn't your dad take baby pictures?"

"No."

"Why not?"

"He doesn't have a camera."

"So what? He's got a cell phone, doesn't he?"

I shook my head.

"Really?" Like it was the craziest thing she'd ever heard. "This is so weird. There's no vacation pictures." Amy wriggled on the sofa, turning over to face me. "Don't you think that's unusual?"

I only shrugged. She was coming close to the edge of our secret life, to things I wasn't supposed to talk about.

"Are there pictures upstairs?"

I shook my head.

"That's *so* weird. I'm going to ask your parents."

"You better not," I told her.

Bumble fell asleep in front of the TV. She was still there when Mom and Dad came back just after seven. Dad headed straight upstairs. He seemed grim and quiet, like he had a headache, but Mom was really happy. She saw Bumble sleeping on the floor and knelt down to kiss her forehead. I turned away before she could do the same thing to me.

"We met all your teachers," she said. "That Mr. Little is *such* a nice man." She looked at Amy. "Everything went well?"

"Yes, Mrs. Watson," said Amy. "They were no trouble."

Mom opened her purse and took out her wallet. She told me, "You're one of his favorites. Did you know that?"

Embarrassed, I shook my head.

"He said you're like a hermit crab that had to be brought out of its shell. He's watched you grow. He's very proud of you."

I saw Amy's little smile and wished Mom would shut up.

"He says you're making friends. You're even chatty now."

Mom counted out money and gave it to Amy.

"Thanks, Mrs. Watson." Amy hoisted her bag onto her shoulder. She started toward the door, then stopped and looked at Mom. "Hey, I was wondering."

Uh-oh, I thought.

In a laughing voice, with a tilt of her head, Amy asked, "Why don't you have any pictures?"

It was like time stopped. Mom's fingers froze on the latch of her purse. Amy kept smiling, like she was expecting a funny story about the kooky Watsons. But Dad stepped into the doorway.

He appeared as suddenly as a psychopath in a horror

movie, and just as creepy. "Now why would you be so worried about that?" he asked.

Amy looked flustered. "I wasn't really *worried*. It just seemed a little strange."

"Oh, I see," said Dad. "Well, maybe we're still unpacking. Did you think of that?"

I doubted she had, as there were no boxes anywhere.

"Or maybe we lost everything in a fire," said Dad. "Or maybe it's just none of your business."

Mom gaped at him, as though she couldn't believe he would say such a thing. Amy turned bright red. "I better go," she said.

Mom went out on the porch to see her off—and maybe to apologize. As soon as they stepped outside, Dad turned on *me*. "What did you tell that girl?" he asked.

"Nothing," I said.

He grunted. "So she pointed out this *bizarre* absence of photographs, and you just sat in stony silence?"

"Why are you mad at *me*?" I asked.

"You're pressing your luck."

"*What?*"

"I don't like how you're changing," he said. "You're becoming bumptious."

"What does that mean?"

"Brash. Arrogant."

Something had happened at school. That was the only way to explain his mood. I spent most of the night wondering what Dad could have seen or heard to make him so suspicious. *He's very proud of you. You're one of his favorites.* No, that couldn't be it. I didn't believe Dad would feel jealous.

You're even chatty now.

Of course that was it. Chatty. It would have terrified Dad to hear that. Suddenly I was sure he'd already decided to take me out of school and was only waiting till morning to tell me. The thought made me so cold inside that I shivered. But when days went by and that didn't happen, I decided to press my luck again.

WALKING TO SCHOOL

On the last Monday in March, I announced that I was walking to school.

I said it straight out while Dad was at the breakfast table with his clown face painted on. He was wearing the whole suit except for the giant wig. Mom was standing at the open front door with the car keys in her hand, ready to give me a ride. I said, "I'm walking to school. Bye."

She was too surprised to move. I was out of the house and down the steps before Dad came running after me with his huge pants swinging around his waist like a bell.

I almost made it to the street. Under the little tree that grew in our front yard, he grabbed my arm.

"Let go," I said, trying to squirm loose.

"Get in the car," he told me.

I twisted away, coming half out of my jacket. "Let go!" I said again.

Dad held the empty sleeve. "If you don't get in the car I'll *put* you in the car."

That would never happen. I pointed up at the apartments, at all the windows and balconies, and told him, "I'll scream."

Dad kind of froze, like a gopher caught by headlights. There was no way in the world he was going to drag a screaming kid into a minivan. Especially not while he was wearing clown clothes.

I pulled my sleeve out of his hand. It flopped between us.

"All right," said Dad. "Will you *please* get in the car? I'll drive you to school and we'll talk about this later."

"No." I hated the disappointed look behind his painted smile, but I couldn't help that. "I'm walking to school."

I strode out to the street and took the shortcut between the buildings. As I passed through the iron gate I was surprised to see Dad's jelly bean car pull up beside me. He must have jumped into it the moment I left and raced up Dead End Road. He must have known the way around.

The passenger window went down with a whirring sound. Dad said, "Get in."

I kept walking.

He drove ahead, stopped, and waited for me to pass. "I won't tell you again," he said. "Get in the car."

It was an empty threat, and we both knew it. So I walked along like he wasn't even there.

"Suit yourself," he said.

The window rolled up again. The minivan crept along behind me, staying exactly a foot behind. If I hurried, Dad drove faster. If I stopped, he waited.

I came to the school from the back, ducking through the narrow gate onto the football field. Dad couldn't possibly follow me there. But he cruised slowly along the fence, tracking me right to the corner where he could see the front steps. And that was where he parked.

Zoe was sitting on the concrete lion, surrounded by the other kids. Someone saw me and shouted, "Hey, it's Igor!" and I saw Angelo turn to look. As I got closer he came out from the group and grabbed me, pretending to wrestle. Zoe said, "Come sit up here."

I wasn't sure I could climb up that pillar. I was shorter than Zoe and not very strong. But she patted the lion and said, "Come on." So I had to try.

I jumped up and grabbed for the top of the pillar. I missed. I tried again and missed again, then managed to dangle by my fingertips while kicking in the air.

Everyone laughed. Even Zoe. I thought it was a disaster, but Angelo stepped up and gave me a boost. The kid who had sworn to kill me actually held out his hands to make a step. He lifted me up, and Zoe grabbed my wrist and swung me the rest of the way, and I landed behind her like a knight on a charger. One of the kids started chanting: *"Ee-gor. Ee-gor."*

I looked over their heads, off to the corner of the school yard, and saw my father the clown leaning against the fence.

He had gotten out of the minivan. He had left the driver's door wide open and cars were jamming up in the street as people tried to swerve around it. I wondered if he had seen me swallowed by the mob of kids and—in a moment of panic—had started running to help me. Now he just stood there in his funny clothes and big bow tie, with his arms spread along the top of the fence. Everyone was staring at him as they passed by, but he didn't move until someone took out a phone to take his picture. Then he hurried back to the van and drove away.

He must have spent all day thinking about it, because there was no jelly bean car waiting to pick me up after school. He might have remembered his stupid dream of building a raft and floating down the Mississippi. He might have just remembered what it's like to be a kid. For sure, something changed his mind.

As soon as Bumble went up to bed, he made me sit down in the living room with him and Mom. "We've been talking," he said, "your mother and I. And she has convinced me to let you walk to school."

"And home again," said Mom, smiling.

"Yes, and home again," said Dad in a grudging way.

"Thanks," I said. "That's great."

"But the rules still hold," said Dad. "Stay on this side of the river. Don't cross Jefferson. And if you're walking, you need to be home by five o'clock."

"When we moved here you said I could stay out until dark," I told him.

"The days are longer now."

"But, Dad—"

"No arguments."

And I didn't argue. Dad had given me more freedom than I'd ever had before.

WHO ARE YOU?

To make sure I followed the rules, Dad went out that night and bought me a watch. He didn't spend very much; it wasn't anything fancy. But when I put it on the next morning and walked out of the house I felt like a prisoner set free after seven years in jail. I took the path between the apartments and the town houses, passing through the iron gate into bright sunshine. It was like I was walking into heaven. And when the day ended I lounged around the concrete lion with the other kids.

The ones with cell phones took them out. They started texting, taking pictures, recording little videos. I had been told since I was small that I should not have my photo "splashed all over the internet," so I automatically looked away, turning my back toward the tiny lenses.

It wasn't really necessary. No one was trying to take *my* picture. Though it made me a little sad to admit it, I was a part of the group only in the way that Pluto was part of the solar system, a distant object circling the edges.

Half an hour later, the ringing and texting and picture-taking had stopped. Only four of us were left: Angelo, Trevis, Zoe, and me. Dented cans didn't have cell phones.

I stood leaning back against the pillar, looking up at the lion's mouth. Someone had smeared red lipstick on the lips and gums, giving it a fierce snarl. Behind me, Angelo said, "Let's go."

I didn't know if he meant to include me. When I turned around, Trevis was already moving, and the two of them walked away. Zoe kept drumming her heels on the lion's ribs, a *bump-a-bump* sound.

"I guess I better get going," I said.

"You want to walk me home?" asked Zoe.

"How far is it?"

"Not far. But if you don't want—"

"Yeah, okay," I said, like it didn't matter to me one way or the other.

"Catch me."

Zoe swung her leg across the lion's shoulders and launched herself from its back. I didn't even have time to lift my hands before she crashed against me. We tumbled backward onto the ground, knocking the wind out of me.

I lay there gasping, but Zoe just laughed and got up. "Nice catch," she said.

We walked north toward Jefferson Street. I had no idea where Zoe lived, but I still had lots of time to get home before five o'clock.

"So why don't you like having your picture taken?" asked Zoe.

"What do you mean?"

"I saw you. The way you turned around when people brought out their phones. You think they'll steal your soul or something?"

"Yeah, right."

"Well, why then?" asked Zoe. "Are you hiding from someone? Are you running away?"

She was only joking—or partly joking—but it scared me that she'd come so close to the truth so quickly.

"Come on, Igor," she said. "You can tell *me*."

I wanted to. What a huge relief it would be to tell her everything. We could sit down, side by side, and I would start with the day when the big policeman had walked into the house with his gun. But I didn't say a word.

Zoe bumped against me and peered into my eyes.

"Who *are* you, Igor Watson?" she asked. "You come out of nowhere with a Spider-Man lunch box. You dress like an old man." Her hand counted off these bizarre things. "You don't want your picture taken. You carry your money in your *sock* . . ." She shook her head. "What planet did you come from?"

"Look who's talking!" I snapped at her without thinking. Words spewed from my mouth by themselves. "You dress like a vampire and you look like a corpse."

Zoe started crying.

I saw her face crumple up, and I felt terrible. I reached out to grab her, but she whirled away and started running.

THE HORRIBLE PLANE CRASH

I got home before five o'clock. But Dad still looked suspicious as he let me in. He stepped onto the porch to make sure no one had followed me, then closed and locked the door.

"Where have you been?" he asked.

"At school," I told him.

"I mean *after* school." He crossed his arms. "What were you doing?"

"Talking with my friends."

"About what?"

"I don't know. Just stuff," I said. "Why does it matter? I came home on time."

He glanced down the hall to see if Mom or Bumble was listening, then lowered his voice. "I don't want to tell your mother yet, but I saw something suspicious."

"Oh, Dad!"

"Shh." He pulled me into the corner and leaned closer. "Listen. I saw the same car go by three times on Jefferson today. Windows dark as a coal mine."

"Maybe they were lost," I said.

"I think whoever was in that car was looking for something. Or for some*one*."

"So we're bugging out?" I said. " 'Cause you saw a car with black windows?"

"No, I don't want to do that." Dad checked to make sure

he'd chained and locked the door. "It might have been some-one lost, as you say. There could be other explanations. I just can't be sure," he said. "But for the next few days I want you to be extra careful. Straight to school, straight home again. All right?"

"Sure, Dad," I said. It was scaring me, the way he was talking.

• • •

That night I thought about Zoe. Again and again in my mind I watched her run away, and I wished I could take back the things I'd said. I decided to tell her I was sorry, but I never got the chance.

The next day, and all that week, she ignored me at school. If I walked toward her, she went the other way. I felt hollow inside, like an empty cave where the wind whistled through. I learned that the only thing worse than not having a friend was *losing* a friend.

At the end of the day on Friday I waited for her at the concrete lion. Angelo was there, and Trevis, and all the cell phone kids. Suddenly the front doors banged open and Zoe strode out.

She came straight down the stairs and right past me. "Wait," I said. On she went, *clomp, clomp, clomp* in her army boots.

"Zoe!"

I started to follow her, but Angelo stopped me. "Forget it," he said.

"Why?"

"That's just Zoe being Zoe."

She turned through the gate and onto the street. Behind me the kids were talking, and their shadows lay on the grass like a big blob with twenty arms and twenty legs. Trevis said, "Hey, Angelo, you wanna do something?"

"Yeah, okay," said Angelo.

He had been leaning against the pillar and now pushed himself up. At the same time, he shoved me with his elbow. "Come on, Igor," he said. "Let's walk up to Deadman's Castle."

I wanted to go with Angelo. I was afraid that if I said no he might never ask again. But I knew I shouldn't. Dad had made that very clear earlier in the week. *Straight to school, straight home again.*

"Well?" asked Angelo. "You wanna go, or not?"

What if Dad was right and the Lizard Man was watching us? Would he really try to grab me in broad daylight? With Angelo and Trevis right beside me? Then I wondered if the Lizard Man could even recognize me. How would he know what I looked like? I'd always been hidden in the car when we bugged out. If we didn't have a garage, Dad would cover my face with a blanket and rush me through the door, into the car, like a criminal on the way to court. For almost all of my life I had lived behind curtains.

Angelo was getting impatient. "You coming?" he said.

I made up my mind. "Sure," I told him.

We walked together out to the street, Angelo and Trevis and me. We turned to the right like marching soldiers, in a line across the sidewalk. Like always, I watched for old men in big cars, for young men in black cars, and all the other things

Dad had told me to watch for. But after a while I began to feel stupid doing that. I was proud to be walking with Angelo. I scuffed my feet like he did. When he put his hands in his pockets, I put my hands in mine.

Trevis found a Coke can and started kicking it ahead of us. It jangled and rattled, skittered and bounced.

"How long have you known Zoe?" I asked Angelo.

He answered with a riddle. "You think anyone knows Zoe?"

The Coke can bounced off a crack in the sidewalk and went spinning along like a top. Angelo stepped over it.

"She keeps changing," he said. "It's like all of a sudden she's got a new name and new clothes and she's acting all weird."

"Why?"

"Who knows?"

Trevis stomped hard on the Coke can. It folded up around his heel and clung to his boot. When he walked he clanked. "It's 'cause of the plane crash. Right, Angelo?"

Angelo only grunted.

"What plane crash?" I asked.

"When she was a little kid," said Trevis. "Tell him, Angelo. She was the only survivor."

"Wow."

"Both of her parents were killed," said Trevis. "Zoe grew up as an orphan. That's why she's weird."

"But I met her mom at the Salvation Army," I said.

"Oh, that's not her real mom. Right, Angelo?" Bored

with the Coke can, Trevis sent it soaring onto somebody's lawn. "It was a 747. A jumbo jet."

We walked half a block and crossed a street. Trevis tossed in another detail. "Three hundred and forty people were killed."

I wondered what it would do to somebody to be the only survivor in a crash like that. If it happened to me, would I start dressing in black and painting my face like a corpse?

Poor Zoe, I thought. "Does she wear all the makeup to hide the scars?"

Trevis started laughing. *Hee-haw, hee-haw.* It belted out of him. I said, "What's so funny?"

"He's making it up," said Angelo. "There was no plane crash. That stuff isn't true." He pushed Trevis sideways, sending him reeling into a hedge. "You can be a real jerk sometimes, Trev."

I would have felt terrible if Angelo had talked to me that way. But Trevis only laughed again. He said, "I bet we see her up at the castle."

"Probably," said Angelo. "She goes there all the time."

"Why?" I asked.

"It's spooky. Like a crip."

I was pretty sure he meant *crypt,* but I didn't correct him.

"Zoe goes in there without a flashlight," he said. "Nobody else will do that."

"You know what?" said Trevis. "Once, she went right to the bottom."

"No she didn't," said Angelo.

"That's what I heard," said Trevis. "She found a secret door down there. Another way out."

"Quit lying!"

"It's the truth!"

They sounded like Mom and Dad on the edge of a fight, each annoyed at the other. But they kept walking toward Jefferson Street.

I knew I should leave them, that I should say "See you later" and turn away to go home. But I just couldn't do it. It was like I was handcuffed to Angelo, or something, and had to go wherever he went. Almost before I knew it, we were on the other side of Jefferson. We walked north for another block, then turned left toward the river. *I'm going to be in so much trouble,* I thought. But I still kept going. I wanted to stay with Angelo. I wanted to see Zoe.

We crossed Dead End Road and kept walking west until we came to a path. A yellow post had been planted in the middle to block motorcycles. Trevis leapfrogged right over it while Angelo and I passed on either side. We walked down a slope to the river, where a spidery bridge made of rope and wood hung high above the water. Only wide enough for one person, it sagged in the middle until it was about twenty feet above the water.

Trevis pushed ahead to be first across. The bridge creaked like an old rocking chair as Angelo went behind him.

This was my very last chance to go home before I had broken every rule that Dad had made. I had not gone straight home. I had crossed Jefferson and was about to cross the river as well. But I still kept going. I couldn't stand the thought of

Angelo talking to me the way he'd talked to Trevis. I followed him onto the bridge.

Out in the middle, Trevis started shifting his weight to make it swing. Angelo and I staggered from side to side.

Hee-haw, laughed Trevis. He threw himself against the ropes and got a rhythm going. The bridge swayed so fast that I had to stop and hold on.

"Quit it!" said Angelo. But Trevis didn't listen. He hauled on the ropes, and they made popping sounds as loud as gunshots. We swung through the air, back and forth.

Angelo swore. "Quit it, Trev! I'm not kidding."

Hee-haw. Trevis threw himself to the left. He threw himself to the right, bouncing off the ropes like an all-star wrestler. I was sure I'd be thrown into the river. Pitched forward and back by the roll of the bridge, I looked down at the water, then up at the sky.

I felt sick.

The blur of trees along the banks, the swirls in the water, the flash of sky made me dizzy. Sure I would puke, I closed my eyes.

Hee-haw. Ropes squealed and banged; the wood groaned.

Angelo was yelling. His voice went high and shrill, and I knew he was terrified. But Trevis kept laughing that stupid laugh, leaning forward and back as he pulled on the ropes.

My feet slipped out from under me. I crumpled onto the planks, tumbled sideways, and the whole world seemed to swing around me.

"Stop it, you moron!" screamed Angelo.

Trevis let go of the ropes. The bridge swayed slower and slower until it came to a rest. "There," he said. "Happy now?"

Angelo helped me up. With an arm around my shoulder he led me back to the path. To me it felt like the bridge was still swinging. I staggered onto the grass, dropped to my knees, and threw up.

Of course Trevis found that hilarious. But Angelo kept his arm around my shoulder and told Trevis again to shut up. "You laugh like a jackass," he said. "Why don't you just get out of here?"

I was glad when Trevis turned and walked away. But I couldn't help feeling sorry for him. Suddenly *he* was the one who didn't belong.

"You okay?" asked Angelo, standing over me.

I nodded. My mouth tasted of sour vomit, and I could feel little chunks clogging my nose. But my dizziness had gone, and I started laughing with Angelo about how we'd both thought the bridge would break, and the way I'd looked when I was throwing up, and what a dork Trevis was.

"Ever since kindergarten he's been like that," said Angelo. "Sometimes I can't stand him."

THE BIG BANG OF FRIENDSHIP

It was an angry Dad who let me into the house. He was waiting at the front door, pulling it open as I crossed the porch. He gave me just enough room to step inside.

"Didn't I tell you to come straight home?" he asked.

"I'm sorry," I said, "but—"

"Did anyone follow you?"

"No," I told him, and that was absolutely true. But still Dad pushed me aside and stared out at the road. Satisfied that no one was there, he locked us safely inside.

"Now let me make this clear," he said. "You're not leaving the house this weekend. Not for a moment."

"But Dad—"

"I don't know what else to do with you." Dad sighed and shook his head. "I give you an inch and you take a mile. I told you to be extra careful, and you paid no attention."

"But nothing happened," I said. "Dad, come on. You saw that one car, and it was days ago. Don't you think it's safe now?"

"No," he said. "It's not that simple."

"Why not?"

"You don't understand."

It was like he had his secrets too. I wondered if I really knew the whole story of the Lizard Man.

I spent that weekend inside the house, and I thought my

dad was really mean. But when enough days went by with
no one being murdered or kidnapped, he relaxed my rules. I
was allowed to stay out until five o'clock again.

. . .

I thought making a friend took a long time, like growing an
acorn into an oak tree. But really it happened fast, like the
big bang theory that Mr. Little had talked about. "For eon
after eon you know nothing but empty darkness," he'd told
us. "Then BOOM! You've got it all."

It was the day at the bridge that made everything different. Angelo stopped hanging around with Trevis and
started hanging around with me instead. Suddenly we were
doing everything together, or as much as we could do before
five o'clock. We started meeting at the same corner every
morning, where an old man lived in a big old house behind a
white fence. If I didn't find Angelo leaning against the fence,
I would lean there myself and wait for him. Sometimes the
old man would come stomping out, yelling, "Get away from
my fence, you hooligan!" We would always laugh about that.
We named him Mr. Meanie.

In room 242, Angelo made Trevis change places, and
we sat together at the back, and every time Mr. Little said
something funny we looked at each other and smiled. And
when the day ended we walked out of the room and down
the hall together. We even went through the big front doors
together, shoving them wide open at the same moment, not
even slowing down. We hung around with the other kids at
the concrete lions, then walked back to Mr. Meanie's fence,
where we said "See ya later" and went our separate ways.

Trevis tagged along at first, always in third place like the way I had been on the day at the bridge. But then he started making other friends, and soon it was only me and Angelo.

We talked all the time, about every crazy thing that came to our minds, like the best way to wrestle an alligator, and what we would do if we were invisible. The only thing we never talked about was the day he'd shoved snow in my face. We sort of pretended it had never happened, that we'd always been friends. That was how it felt.

I even made friends with Zoe again. She went from saying nothing at all to saying two or three words at a time: *"Move over." "Shut up, loser."* After a while her sentences got longer, and soon it was like she'd never been mad at me.

I came to see that kids in middle school acted the same way as countries. They could go from friends to enemies and back again. But they could also go to war for a hundred years.

· · ·

It was near the end of April when I went to Angelo's house for the first time. He took me there after school.

I didn't expect a mansion. But his place was more ordinary than I'd imagined. A small, square house with small, square windows, it looked like the sort of house Bumble always drew, but without the jet of smoke shooting from the chimney.

When Angelo opened the door I smelled garlic and spices. He shouted, "Ma! I'm home," and I heard the scrabbling sound of claws.

"Here comes Smasher," said Angelo.

I stepped back, expecting a pit bull to come charging down

the hall, or a boxer with a chest wider than mine. But around the corner, scrabbling on its little legs, came the funniest dog I'd ever seen. Smasher was no bigger than a cat, a black-and-white bundle of fur with floppy ears and a scrunched-up face that looked a bit like Angelo's. Her front teeth showed in a jagged line, like she was smiling. She hopped while she ran, kind of skipping along, then twirled little circles at Angelo's feet.

He got down on his knees and hugged her. Smasher panted, snorted, squirmed in his arms. She stretched her neck to lick his nose.

Behind her came Angelo's mother, like a snowman stuffed in a yellow dress with big red roses all over it. She called Angelo *patatino*. "Ah, there's my *patatino*," she said. "And who's this?"

"Igor, Ma."

"Hello, Igor!" She pinched my face with her thumbs, smiling so warmly that I could only smile right back. "Doesn't he look like your uncle Paolo?"

"Ma, Uncle Paolo's eighty years old," said Angelo.

"Well, when he was a boy," she told him.

"Yeah, okay," said Angelo. "We're going upstairs, Ma."

"You want something to eat?"

"Not just now."

With Smasher running laps around Angelo's feet, we walked through a living room that looked like a museum. There were red chairs with thick seats, lamps with enormous shades, oil paintings in clunky frames. A grandfather clock ticked away the time with a pendulum the size of a shovel, and a crucified Jesus watched sadly over all of it.

"Nobody ever sits in here," said Angelo. "Not since my dad died."

Upstairs, his bedroom made me jealous. On a table stood a huge TV, on a desk a big computer and an iPad. He had a hockey stick and a baseball glove, a football and a Frisbee, and shelves full of toys that he probably hadn't touched in years.

"Come on, Smash," said Angelo. He flopped across his bed, and the little dog sprang up beside him. I realized why it had such a funny way of moving.

"Your dog's only got three legs," I said.

"Yeah, she used to have four," said Angelo. "Then she got hit by a car." He held her up with his arms straight, like he was bench-pressing her.

"What kind of a dog is she?" I asked.

"Sort of a mixture." Angelo laughed as she squirmed in his hands. "She's mostly a bloodhound."

"She doesn't *look* like a bloodhound," I said.

"You should see how she tracks. It's like the Manhunter."

I didn't know what he meant. I didn't ask.

Angelo bent his arms, lowering the dog until he could kiss her. She kissed him back with her pink, fluttering tongue, and I thought that if I'd seen that on my first day at school I would never have been afraid of Angelo.

He looked over at me. "You like *Medal of Honor?*"

"What's that?"

"A video game, you loser."

With a shake of his head, Angelo set up the game on PlayStation. He had a character named Johnny Shiloh. "He's like a war hero," Angelo told me. "I've had him two years and he's never been killed." For me, Angelo made a character named Bob.

I was hopeless. Poor Bob never lasted more than five minutes, and every time he came to life again he died again. But Angelo was amazing. He *became* Johnny Shiloh, running and crawling and somersaulting across the battlefield. He kept telling me where the enemy was hiding, because he'd played the game a million times, and the room shook with the sounds of our battle.

I lost track of time. The next thing I knew, Angelo's mother was shouting up the stairs that supper was almost ready.

"Okay, Ma!" yelled Angelo. On the screen, Johnny Shiloh was racing across a bridge. Angelo cried, "Look out behind you!"

There was a blare of machine-gun sounds. The controller started vibrating in my hands, and Bob died again.

I checked my watch. It was 5:59. "Oh, no!" I said. "I have to go home."

"Call your mom." Johnny Shiloh sprinted across a street and leapt onto a pile of rubble. Angelo kept twisting the controller in his hand, clicking the buttons like crazy. "Tell her you're staying for supper."

"I can't."

"Why not?"

"We don't have a phone."

Angelo was so surprised that he looked away from the game. In that moment, Johnny Shiloh got shot. The screen turned red with oozing blood, and the little man who'd fought for two years, who had won ten thousand battles, lay dying on a painted street.

"No!" said Angelo. *"Noooo!"* He pressed every button; he pushed every lever. He was like a doctor working with medical machines, trying to save Johnny Shiloh. I could hear the humming throb of his controller, a heartbeat slowing down. Then the game ended.

Angelo groaned. "He's gone. Johnny Shiloh's dead!"

He dropped his controller and lay back with his arm over his eyes. Smasher sprang up to lick his face, but Angelo pushed her away.

"I'm sorry," I said.

"Forget it." Smasher kept lunging at him, whining and licking, and Angelo fended her off. "So why don't you have a phone?" he asked. "I thought everyone had a phone."

"Well, my mom has one but—"

"Then call *that* one."

"It doesn't have a number."

"Every phone has a number," said Angelo.

"Not my mom's. It's a special phone."

"Yeah, sure," said Angelo. He didn't believe me, and I didn't blame him. He said, "If you don't want to call her, just say so."

"No, it's true," I said. "She's a telemarketer. She's got a phone that lets her call people, but no one can call her. It doesn't have a number or something. I don't know, but it can't be traced. Not even by the CIA."

"Really?" asked Angelo.

"That's what my dad says."

"Wow. That's crazy."

Wait till you hear the rest, I thought.

Downstairs, Mrs. Bonito shouted again. "Angelo, it's on the table!"

"Okay, Ma!" He lowered his voice. "If I don't eat now she'll kill me."

His mom was disappointed that I wasn't staying for dinner. "I made noodles," she said.

"Ma, you mean *oodles,*" said Angelo. "But he's gotta go."

"You want to take some with you?" she asked.

"No, thank you," I said. Then she pinched my cheeks again, and Angelo took me to the door.

"See you, Watson," he said as he let me out.

So I said, "Yeah, see you, Bonito," and set off for home.

I ran all the way to Dead End Road. I went up the steps two at a time, across the porch in a bound. As I reached the door the letter slot opened. "It's Igor!" shouted Bumble.

Everyone came to meet me. Mom stood in the background, touching her eyes with a dish towel. Dad's old makeup gave him a creepy smile. He said, "Come in."

"I'm sorry I'm late," I told him. "I was—"

"I *know* where you were."

I didn't believe him; it seemed impossible. Still, I felt a little shiver, a hint of the fear that my dad always knew when I was doing something wrong.

"You'll be staying around home next weekend," said Dad. "You're grounded again."

MY CRAZY DAD

The next morning, I got to Mr. Meanie's house before Angelo did. I leaned against the fence to wait, kind of hoping the old man would come out and yell at me. But he didn't. When I saw Angelo shambling up the street with his hands in his pockets, I knew something was wrong.

He didn't say hi like he normally did. He didn't smile or punch my arm. He kept looking at the ground as we walked toward school.

I said, "What's new, *patatino?*"

"Don't call me that," he said. "You have to be an Italian mother to use that word."

"What does it mean?"

" 'Little potato.' "

It made me laugh. But Angelo was silent and serious. We were nearly at the school before he spoke again.

"Your dad's a nut," he said. "He called my mom yesterday. Just after you left."

So what Dad had said was true. *I know where you were.* But how he had figured it out was a mystery. "What did he say?" I asked.

"A lot," said Angelo. "Mom picked up the phone and here's this guy yelling at her. '*Where's my son?*' "

"I guess he was worried," I said.

"He wanted to know where we live. He was going to come to the house," said Angelo. "But Ma told him you'd already gone."

"How did he know who to call?" I asked. "How did he get your number?"

"I don't know," said Angelo. "But he's a little bit scary, and a whole lot crazy."

I learned the rest of the story in gym class. I was sitting on the changing bench when Mr. Moran came out of his office with his silver whistle hanging around his neck. He put on his red hat, then twisted it back and forth to make it comfortable.

I shouted, "Are we going inside or outside, sir?"

A few people laughed. Everyone waited for Mr. Moron to tell me, "Look at the hat!"

But this time he just motioned with his thumb. "Into the sin bin, Igor."

I had to get up and walk past him. Then he followed me into the office and closed the door. Outside, the boys were whispering.

"I expect that sort of thing from Trevis and the others," said Mr. Moran. "I thought you were better than them. Guess I was wrong."

I felt awful.

He took off his hat, tossed it onto the desk, and sat in his big swivel chair. "Everything all right at home, Igor?"

I could barely mumble, "Yes, sir."

"Did your father tell you he talked to me yesterday?"

"No," I said. That explained everything.

"He came to the school lookin' for you. Guess he was drivin' around, lookin' everywhere. I was out on the field with the baseball team. He came up to me. Asked if I knew you."

Mr. Moran clasped his hands together and leaned forward. "He wanted to know who your friends were. Where you go after school. What sort of things you get up to. I told him I don't know much about you. Except you're a good kid. Used to keep to yourself, and now you chum around with the Bonito boy."

Mr. Moran sighed and spread his hands apart. "Your father seemed . . . I don't know—off the wall. I told him, 'Your boy's probably playin' ball.' But he said, '*My* boy doesn't play ball.' He said, '*My* boy should be doing what he's told.'"

That sounded like Dad, all right.

"He came in here to use my phone. Had to call the Bonito place right then. Couldn't wait another minute." Mr. Moran stood up and put on his hat again. "You're growin' up, Igor. Findin' your feet. If your father can't accept that, well, that's his lookout. Don't let him stuff you back in a sack."

He opened the office door. "Just keep in mind he cares about you. Has a funny way of showin' it, but he does."

FOUR-RING CIRCUS

It was the second week of May when Bumble had her birthday. Mom made the traditional birthday supper that she called the four-ring circus. Arranged together on my plate were all of Bumble's favorite foods—two fish sticks, a slice of meatloaf, and a scoop of macaroni, all piled on a frozen waffle.

"Oooh, boy, the foreign circus!" said Bumble.

Supper was followed by a chocolate cake with five candles burning on top. As Mom put it down in front of a grinning Bumble, she said, "Make a wish, Bumblebee."

I remembered my last birthday wish, that the Lizard Man would find us. It seemed like a silly idea that I'd had long ago. Bumble scrunched up her eyes and said, "I wish we never bug out."

Mom smiled. "So do I."

"I want to live here happily forever after," said Bumble.

She knelt on her chair, leaned on the table, and blew out the candles—all five in one breath. They were still smoking when Mom plucked them from the cake and started cutting slices.

"You know, I had my doubts at first," she said. "But it's turned out well. I feel more at home than I've ever felt before. It's a good place."

"It's a great place," I said.

"It's the best place ever," said Bumble.

We looked at Dad, expecting a little speech. He was fiddling with his fork, tapping the tines on the table.

"Don't you like it here, Dad?" asked Bumble.

The fork twirled slowly through his fingers like a tiny baton. He said, "We can't afford to become complacent."

"What's come placement?" asked Bumble.

"Complacent," Dad corrected her. "Blind to danger."

"Oh, honey," said Mom. "You said we'd be safe here. Don't you think we can relax a little bit?"

"I do not." Dad laid the fork flat and set it perfectly straight on his napkin. "As a matter of fact, I've been thinking it might be time to move on."

"No!" wailed Bumble. She kicked the table hard enough to rattle our water glasses, then crossed her arms and scowled.

I thought I could help if I told my own story. I said, "It's like Angelo."

"Oh?" said Dad in his sarcastic voice. "And just how, exactly, is this like *Angelo*?"

"I used to be scared of him."

Mom gaped. "Your friend?"

"Yes, Mom." I told them about my second morning at Rutherford B. Hayes, about Angelo being a bully. I explained how I'd thought I'd be safe if I kept running away.

"You see, Dad?" I said. "I never should have been scared, 'cause he wasn't really going to kill me. He just wanted me to *think* he would kill me."

"I get your point," said Dad. "But you—"

"A bully's like a dog that chases cats," I said. "He does it for fun, until the cat fights back. Then he stops. If you stand up to a bully you see that he's not all that scary after all."

Dad picked up his fork again and turned it end over end.

I said, "My teacher Mr. Moran says you have to go in and play the game. If you hold back you feel safe. But you can't win until you go in and take your shots. A bully never stops."

"Neither do you, apparently."

I felt like he'd slapped me.

"Look," said Dad. "You're twelve years old. You think you know everything, but you don't. Angelo being a bully has nothing to do with our situation. You have no idea what's really going on."

"Then tell me," I said.

He shook his head. "The less you know, the better."

ASKING THE FOLKS

The days became sunny and hot. Behind the yellow house, the river grew so shallow that sandbars began to appear. If I'd been allowed to do it, I could have walked right across.

I loved the warm weather. Like all the boys in my class, I wore T-shirts all the time, and my arms turned from skinny white pipes to skinny brown pipes. The girls wore colorful little blouses—except for Zoe. Looking stranger than ever, she still strode through the school in her long black coat.

I was walking home with Angelo on a Friday when he asked me to stay overnight at his house.

"I got a new game," he said. "It's like *Medal of Honor* but even better. You can fry people with a flamethrower! You can see their skin melt."

I thought that sounded horrible, but Angelo's eyes glowed like little lamps. "We could play all night. We could play till *dawn.*"

"Cool." I didn't tell Angelo I had never stayed up after midnight.

"Come over tomorrow," he said. "You can go home on Sunday."

"I'll ask my folks." I called them folks now, because that was what Angelo called them.

"Ask your mom," he said. "Don't ask your dad. He's a dork."

Angelo still hadn't met either of my folks. Everything he knew he'd learned from me, and I felt bad about the things I'd said. "He just worries a lot," I told Angelo. "He likes to know what's going on."

"Yeah, he's a control freak. Let's go ask your mom right now before he gets home."

We took the shortcut and found the minivan parked in the driveway. Angelo said, "Your dad must be home."

"No, he walks to work," I said. "But he *could* be home; I don't know."

"I'll wait for you here."

Angelo walked over and leaned against the spindly poplar tree in our front yard. He never stood up straight if there was something to lean against.

I went to the house and knocked on the door. *Tap-tap-tap. Tap-tap-tap.* When Bumble looked out at me through the letter slot I told her, "Get Mom."

Thomas the Tank Engine was babbling away in the living room. Upstairs, the shower was running. Mom had to come from the kitchen to let me in. As I came through the door she turned around and went right back there.

I trailed behind her. "Is it okay if I sleep over at Angelo's tomorrow?" I asked.

"Just a minute; I'm in the middle of something." Mom sat in her chair by the spy phone and started writing in her book. Upstairs, the shower stopped; the door banged. I imagined Dad reaching for a towel, wrapping it around his waist. I wanted to get out of the house before he came downstairs and started asking questions.

"Mom, Angelo's waiting," I told her.

She held up a hand, wrote a few more words, then closed the book. "All right," she said. "Now what were you asking?"

"Can I sleep over at Angelo's house tomorrow?"

"I don't see why not," said Mom. "But you'd better ask your father."

"Well, forget it then," I said.

"Why?"

"He'll say no."

"I wasn't aware you could predict the future," said Mom.

"He *always* says no," I told her. "He just wants to wreck my life."

"I don't believe that's his goal," said Mom. "He—"

"Could *you* ask him? Please?"

"No," she said. "I'm sorry. You'll have to ask him yourself." She pulled her headset over her ears. "Here he comes now."

Dad was practically galloping down the stairs. I had never heard him move so fast, and I turned to talk to him. But he didn't come into the kitchen. The front door banged open and he went thundering across the porch.

Mom tried to peer around the doorway. "What's he *doing?*"

We heard him shout. "Stay right there!"

In the moment it took me to reach the front door, Dad had already grabbed Angelo by the collar. They were standing under the little tree, a crazy-looking man in a bathrobe shaking a frightened kid. Dad kept shouting. "What are you doing here? What's your name?"

I ran across the lawn. Dad's bathrobe flapped around his hairy legs, and Angelo was crying.

I felt awful to see him like that, kind of dangling at the end of Dad's arm. His fists flailed at nothing; his eyes squirted tears. I pulled at Dad's bathrobe and shouted, "Leave him alone! He's my friend, Dad. That's Angelo."

Dad looked confused. "Why's he lurking around the house?"

"He's waiting for me."

Dad let go. Angelo took off like a rabbit.

"Wait!" I shouted. But he kept running, and I could understand that. If it was me, I would want to find a quiet, private place to straighten my clothes and wipe my tears away. I would never let on that anything had happened.

"Why couldn't he walk up to the door like a normal person?" asked Dad, like it was all Angelo's fault.

" 'Cause he's scared of you," I said.

"Why?" Dad looked completely puzzled. Across the street, Angelo went scurrying into the shortcut.

"You don't trust anybody," I said. "You're so mean sometimes."

Dad looked up at the apartment buildings, then back toward the house, where Mom was standing at the door. Like he suddenly realized he was wearing only his bathrobe, Dad tightened the belt and walked quickly up the path.

At the door Mom asked him sarcastically, "Have a nice talk with Angelo?"

Dad pushed past and started up the stairs.

"I hope you're happy with yourself," she said, her voice

rising to follow him. "You just drove away your son's best friend. I doubt we'll ever see *him* again."

Dad stopped at the landing. "Well, he shouldn't have been acting like a thief," he said. Under the red bathrobe, the backs of his legs were as white as bowling pins. "I look out the window and see someone lurking under a tree, what am I *supposed* to think?"

"That he's shy?" asked Mom. "Do you know what he wanted? He came to ask if Igor could sleep over at his house. And you—"

"All right, I'll do it your way," said Dad. "I'll close my eyes and pretend everything's fine."

He stomped up the rest of the stairs and slammed the bedroom door. Mom sighed. "Don't be mad at him," she said. "I really think he's trying his best."

THE SLEEPOVER

Mom called Angelo's mother to arrange for the sleepover. On Saturday afternoon I stuffed a few things into a plastic bag and said, "I'll see you tomorrow."

Dad tried to give me another lecture about the need to stay alert. "Don't let your guard down," he said. "This is important."

It looked like he was getting ready to talk for a long time. But Mom stepped between us and gave me a small box wrapped in fancy paper. "For Mrs. Bonito," she said. "A little thank-you."

I was happy when I left the house. But only halfway along the path to the iron gate I began to feel afraid. In my whole life I had never spent a night away from home. What if I got lonely? The farther I went, the more my fear kept building. What if the Lizard Man arrived while I was gone, and I went home on Sunday to find a deserted house? I decided that I didn't really want to be away from home all night. But as soon as I knocked on Angelo's door and Mrs. Bonito greeted me, my worries vanished.

"Holy smackerels, my favorite boy," she said.

She was wearing a different dress, but it still had flowers printed on it, like all her clothes were made from old sofas. She beamed at me.

Smasher came scampering down the stairs, crazy with excitement. Angelo shouted from his room, "Watson?"

"Yeah!" I shouted back.

"Come on up."

I took Mom's present out of the bag and gave it to Mrs. Bonito. She almost started bawling. "The nicest thing," she said. Then she pinched my cheeks and sent me upstairs. "You know the way."

Up in Angelo's room, I found him setting up the game. He was looking at the TV, watching my reflection. "So they let you out," he said.

I nodded. "My dad's not too happy about it."

"Your dad's a freak."

Angelo pressed some buttons on his controller, and the game came on. He had already made up two characters: for him another Johnny Shiloh, for me a guy called Colt Cabana.

"Where'd you get that name?" I asked.

"From all-star wrestling," said Angelo. "Me and my dad used to watch Colt Cabana every Saturday morning. We lay on the couch and ate potato chips."

That was more than he'd ever told me about his dad. But he didn't say anything else. We started playing the game as Smasher lay on the bed with her ears twitching. Johnny Shiloh and Colt Cabana conquered Iwo Jima, with Angelo giving the orders: "Look behind you!" "Take the point!" When I went hand to hand with an enemy soldier, Angelo called out Colt Cabana's favorite wrestling moves. "Eat the feet!" and "Give him the Frankensteiner!"

It was one of the greatest times ever. But we didn't stay up until dawn. At nine o'clock we turned off the lights and told ghost stories in the dark, using a flashlight to make our faces look like fiery skulls. At eleven, Angelo said he was tired, and he turned on the lights again and brought out an old sleeping bag with a tartan lining. He tossed it on the floor.

It looked about as soft as a brick, and I wasn't looking forward to sleeping there. But Angelo surprised me. "You can have the bed," he told me. "That'll be the rule. Whoever sleeps over gets the bed."

I sat on the mattress to take off my shoes. By mistake I pulled off my sock as well, and the hundred-dollar bill sprang out. It landed beside Angelo, a little wad of green paper.

"What's that?" he asked.

I bent down to grab it. But Smasher was faster. She snatched it up in her mouth and shook it furiously.

"Drop that," I said.

She growled. She snarled. Her eyes shone crazily. When I tried to pry open her little jaws she pulled back her lips and growled even louder.

"Ow!" I said. "She bit me."

Angelo found that hilarious. He tapped a finger on Smasher's black button nose and told her, "Drop it." But she only growled at him and wouldn't let go of the money until Angelo wrestled it out of her mouth.

I reached out my hand. "Give it back, Angelo."

But he rolled away and started unfolding my money. By then it was soaked with dog spit, and he had to peel the layers apart. First the phone number appeared, written in huge indelible writing, then the face of Benjamin Franklin.

"A hundred dollars!" said Angelo.

"Come on, give it back," I told him.

"Okay!" He tossed the money at me. "I wasn't going to steal it."

I shoved it into in my sock, pulled the sock over my foot, and slid into bed. Angelo asked, from the floor, "Why do you have a hundred dollars in your sock?"

I felt like our whole friendship depended on what I said. If I lied, he would know it. So I told just enough of the truth to make sense. "Oh, that's my dad. You know what he's like. Everyone should carry money for an emergency."

"In their *socks?*"

I shrugged. "You can't lose it."

"Well, *he's* lost it," said Angelo. "Good night."

He turned off the lights and crawled into the sleeping bag. Without anyone saying anything, we invented our second rule: at sleepovers we slept in our socks and our jeans and our T-shirts. I heard Smasher wriggle in beside Angelo.

"So what's the phone number?" he asked. "On the money."

I stared into the dark and said, "I don't know."

"Yes you do." In Angelo's voice was a hint—just a little hint—of the bullying boy he had been at first.

"No, really," I told him. "I don't know." And that was the absolute truth. "Dad wrote it down when he gave me the money. He told me to call it if I ever need help."

"So it's like the bat signal?"

"Yes, Angelo," I said. "It's like the bat signal."

THE RULES OF FRIENDSHIP

Just like there were rules about sleepovers, there were rules about friendship too. Some were so obvious that even *I* knew them. If Angelo invited me to sleep over at his house, I had to invite him to sleep over at mine.

But I didn't want to do that. I was afraid of what he'd think of Mom and Bumble, or that he'd get bored in my empty room and go home early. Either way, he would tell everyone at school what a loser I was, and we would never be friends again.

But the rules of friendship had to be followed.

My last hope was that Dad would say no. But without even thinking about it, he nodded and said, "Sure. Sounds like a good idea."

"He has a dog," I said, thinking that would change his mind. "A *little* dog."

"Oh, really?" Dad's face scrunched up. He hated dogs in general, but especially little dogs like Smasher. He called them rats in fur coats, thinking it was hilarious. He said, "Do you think Angelo could leave it at home?"

"No," I said.

Dad sighed. "Well, I suppose it will be all right."

I didn't believe that Dad was trying to be generous or anything. He just thought it would be easier to watch over me if he kept me close to home.

Angelo showed up at noon on Saturday. I heard Smasher barking as I unfastened the chain and turned the lock. As soon as I opened the door she darted inside, leapt up to greet me, and bounded into the kitchen.

I heard Dad's voice—"What's *that?*"—and then an excited squeal from Bumble. I walked into the room to find my sister on the floor, with Smasher squirming upside down to get her belly tickled. Mom gushed. "Oh, what a cute dog!"

Dad watched with a sour frown. He didn't look any happier when Angelo came into the room.

I had never brought anyone home before, and nobody knew what to say or how to act. Mom seemed especially flustered, like a bird that had flown into the house by mistake. I said, "This is Angelo," and she bobbed her head and twittered, "How do you do?"

It was awkward for Angelo. He stood there holding his sleeping bag stuffed in its sack, with the end of his toothbrush sticking out of his shirt pocket.

But it was even more awkward for Dad. Pretending they'd never met, he shook hands and smiled so horribly that I could see all of his teeth and his gums as well. With faded clown paint on his cheeks, he looked stranger than ever.

Bumble was shy. She went away and brought Hideous George, holding him out in front of her for Angelo to admire.

Angelo told me, "I didn't know you had a brother."

"Oh, ha-ha," I said.

We went upstairs. Naturally, Bumble came with us, scampering on her hands and knees behind Smasher. I tried to hold her back with my foot as I closed the bedroom door, but she started wailing. Angelo said, "Aw, let her in."

Bumble gave me a dirty look, then climbed up on my bed and bounced on the mattress. Angelo was gazing around the room in a way that made me feel embarrassed. I imagined what he was thinking. *No video games? No computer? How can anyone live like this?*

He went to the side window facing the park and pulled the curtains open.

"You shouldn't do that!" shouted Bumble.

"Why not?"

" 'Cause we're not s'posed to."

Angelo looked at me strangely again. "You're not supposed to open the curtains?"

"Dad doesn't want people looking in," I told him.

"Crazy." He let the curtains fall shut and went to the other window, to look out on the river. He had to lean over the bed to move the curtains; then the first thing he noticed was the roof over the little back porch. "Can you get out onto there?" he asked. "Can you climb down?"

"I don't know," I said.

"You never tried?" Angelo got onto the bed and tried to push up the window. But it didn't move. He banged with his fist till the glass made crackling sounds. "It's painted shut," he said. "You got a knife?"

"No."

I didn't know why he bothered to ask me. From his pocket he pulled out a little penknife with a bone handle. He snapped it open and started scraping at the wood. Old dead flies and flakes of yellow paint fell to the sill.

When Angelo tried the window again it made a terrible screech that I was sure Mom and Dad would hear downstairs. But nobody came running to see what we were doing, and he soon had it sliding up and down with barely a sound at all. When he folded the knife and put it back in his pocket, the window was moving so easily that he could push it open with his fingertip. He held it open and started climbing over the sill.

Bumble scolded him. "You're not allowed to do that! I'm telling Dad."

Angelo already had one foot out on the roof. He looked back and said, "You better not. This is a secret, and you know what happens if you tell a secret?"

Bumble shook her head.

"You shrivel up and die. Just like those old flies. Tell her, Igor."

"That's right," I said.

Bumble bit her lip as she stared at the dead flies on windowsill. She looked very solemn.

"Why don't you go stand guard?" said Angelo. "Tell us if you see someone coming."

Bumble couldn't move fast enough. She rolled herself off the bed and leapt to her feet. Looking just like a tiny Dad, she stood pressed against the door, peering through a crack.

Angelo climbed out onto the roof. Smasher stood up on her one hind leg, holding on to the sill as she watched him, her tail wagging furiously. Ivy crunched under his feet as Angelo crept to the edge and leaned over.

"We could get down here easily," he said. "There's kind of a trellis."

I thought of Mom underneath us in the kitchen. I said, "You better come in."

But Angelo knelt by the trellis and tested the ivy. "It's pretty strong," he said. "I'm gonna climb down."

"Don't," I told him.

Dad called up the stairs. "Igor? What are you boys doing?"

"Come back inside," I told Angelo.

The ivy shifted under his knees. He teetered at the edge, grabbing at the ivy to save himself.

Smasher yelped. She tried to jump out onto the roof, leaping at the sill until she jolted the window loose. It slammed shut with a bang that scared her.

Bumble said, "Someone's coming up the stairs!"

I tried to push the window open again, but the latch had jammed. I had to fiddle with it while Angelo crawled up the roof toward me.

"It's Dad!" yelled Bumble.

"Shh." I turned the latch. I pushed the window up and reached out to pull Angelo closer.

"He's at the top of the stairs!"

Angelo leaned in through the window. Smasher fell aside as he tumbled onto the bed. I swept the curtains closed behind him just as Bumble screamed, "He's here!"

The door swung wide open and Dad walked in. He looked

at Angelo on the bed, at Smasher wriggling upside down, at me just standing there. "What are you boys doing?" he asked.

"Nothing, Mr. Watson," said Angelo.

"You're not going out on the roof, are you?"

"Oh, no," said Angelo, as innocent as a choirboy. "That would be dangerous."

Dad knew the truth. I could see it in his eyes. But all he said was "You're right. You'd break your necks."

A WHISTLING LOON

"*There's nothin' to* do here," said Angelo on Sunday morning.

I had been right to worry.

"Why don't you have any video games?" he asked as he sprawled on the bed with Smasher. "Why don't you have a computer?"

"My dad doesn't like stuff like that," I said.

"Why? 'Cause he thinks they rot your brain?"

"He thinks people can use them to spy on you."

"Through a *video game*? Is he nuts?" The bed creaked as Angelo rolled over to look out through the curtains. "We should go to Deadman's Castle."

I would do almost anything to stop him from going home early, but that didn't seem like a good idea. "I better not," I said.

"Why?" asked Angelo. "You're allowed to go out, aren't you?"

I didn't realize he was teasing me. "Sure," I said. "But I've got rules."

"Like what?"

"I'm not supposed to cross Jefferson."

"You've already done that. We went—"

"I know," I said. "But I'm not supposed to. And I'm not allowed to go on the other side of the river."

"Are you serious, Watson?"

"Yeah, kind of."

He laughed. "I bet your folks go there."

"Probably," I said.

"So why shouldn't *you*?"

That was a good question.

"You wanna go right now?"

"Where?"

"Across Jefferson Street and over the river to Deadman's Castle," said Angelo, like I was stupid. "Stay with the program, Watson."

"I don't know," I said.

"You scared?"

"No." But that was a lie. I was afraid of getting in trouble with Dad again.

"Then let's do it."

I shrugged and said, "Sure." Like I didn't care one way or the other.

Angelo sat up on the bed. "Let's go out the window. We can climb down the ivy." All of a sudden he was Johnny Shiloh. "Get your sister to distract your folks. I'll go first and you can lower Smasher to me. I'll give you a signal. Like a whistling loon."

He cupped his hands together and blew between his thumbs, making a low whistle that was more like a duck than a loon.

"Why don't we just go out the front door?" I asked.

"Okay. Whatever," said Angelo.

When we went downstairs it was Dad who came to let us out. "Where are you heading?" he asked.

"We're just going for a walk."

"Well, okay," said Dad, grumbling. "You know the rules."

As soon as we were out of the house Angelo started asking questions. As little Smasher wove from side to side in front of us, he grilled me about my dad. "Where does he work?"

"At Fun and Games," I said.

"Really?" said Angelo. Then he made the connection. "He's that guy in the clown clothes, isn't he?"

"Yeah."

"And he walks to work? In his clown suit?"

"Yeah." Dad wore those clothes to work, and he wore them home. If he had shopping to do on the way, he did that in his clown suit too. Hardly anyone on Dead End Road had ever seen him without it.

"Wow, that's weird," said Angelo.

Smasher chased butterflies that rose from little white flowers, while big clouds tumbled along above us. It was a beautiful day and I didn't want to waste it talking about my father. But Angelo kept asking questions. How long had Dad been working at Fun and Games? What did he do before that?

"He ran a hardware store," I said, slipping into the old lie that I knew so well.

"Where?"

"In Greenaway."

"Where's that?"

"Oh, it's a small town," I said.

"Yeah, but what state's it in?"

And suddenly I had a feeling I'd told him the story before.

But I couldn't remember for sure, or what state I might have named. Stupidly, I said, "I dunno."

"You don't know what state you lived in?"

"We've moved a hundred times," I said.

"I thought you lived there all your life."

So I *had* told him the story. Or he'd heard it from Zoe, or from somebody else who had heard it from her. I remembered Dad telling me that I couldn't build a friendship based on lies, and now I understood why. I saw it crumbling apart.

"So what state's Greenaway in?" asked Angelo again.

He just wouldn't give up. He was like Smasher with something fixed in her mouth, shaking it every which way. I said, "I'm not supposed to talk about it."

"Why?"

"Please, Angelo."

"Okay." He shrugged. "I don't care."

But he did. I could tell by the tone of his voice, by the way he turned his head aside. We kept walking, but everything felt different. I was afraid something had changed between us.

WHAT IT'S LIKE TO BE DEAD

"Crossing Jefferson," announced Angelo as we stepped out onto that street. "I hope we make it back alive."

I wasn't sure if he was poking fun at me or at my dad. But I actually did feel a bit nervous. As I'd always been warned to do, I watched for an old man in a big car. But this time it wasn't the Lizard Man I worried about. I watched for *my* old man in a bright green minivan.

Angelo said Smasher would lead us right to Deadman's Castle. "She could get there blindfolded," he said. When she turned through the gate to a cemetery, he told me she was taking a shortcut. We followed her between the tombstones.

Walking on graves gave me the creeps. I hated the shallow dents in the grass, knowing what lay underneath. But Angelo didn't care, and to Smasher it was just a place to chase squirrels. They bolted ahead of her, up the trunks of gnarly old trees.

The tombstones were moss-covered, ancient and broken. I saw an angel with a clipped wing, a cross with a shattered arm. I saw that someone had put the wrong head on one of the cherubs. And then I saw Zoe lying flat on a grave, and my heart missed a beat.

She was dressed in her long black coat. Flat on her back, she lay with her feet together, toes pointing up, arms stiff at her sides. Her hair made a black pool around her head, like old blood, and she looked more than ever like a corpse. But as we came closer her head turned, and she called out in a cheery voice, "Hi! Where are you guys going?"

"Up to the castle," said Angelo.

"Cool. I'll go with you."

She rose from the grave like a zombie. Then she brushed bits of grass from her clothes, and we walked together out of the cemetery. A faint tinkling came from her jewelry.

"What were you doing there?" I asked.

"Practicing," she said. "I wanted to know what it's like to be dead."

Half a block farther, Angelo finally asked, "So what was it like?"

"Kind of boring," said Zoe.

We came to the path with a yellow post in the middle and crossed the river on the swinging bridge. A hill appeared in the distance as the road turned to the right. It looked like a toad, green and lumpy, with a flat top made of mounds of bare rock.

"That's Deadman's Castle up there," said Angelo.

A broken arch poked up from the rocky summit. Seeing it made my skin turn prickly. All of a sudden, on that warm day, I was shivering.

I was pretty sure I'd been here before.

In my mind I could see myself as a little kid, trudging through snow toward that shape on the hilltop. On my hands were red mittens made of wool, and little burrs of snow clung to their backs. I remembered the cold tang on my lips, and the taste of wet wool, as I bit off the tiny snowballs.

As we walked toward the hill, we passed things that I sort of recognized: a small park with a sandbox and rusted climbing bars; a fence made of iron spikes shaped like arrowheads.

"I think I've been here before," I said.

"Not with me," said Zoe.

"I know that," I said. "It's a feeling."

Angelo laughed. "Watson, you're weird."

In a sort of flash, I knew what I'd find around the next bend in the road. I said, "We're coming to Sandy's."

"What's *Sandy's?*" asked Angelo.

"The store around the corner." I could picture it clearly, a little wooden building with a blue awning. If I went inside, a woman who looked like an old witch would sell me candy out of big glass jars.

Angelo said, "There's no store, Watson."

How could that be? I remembered buying jawbreakers there, and trying to make one of them last all the way home. It clicked against my teeth, and every now and then I pulled it out to see how much was left and what color it had turned to. By the time I got home it was a tiny thing no bigger than a poppy seed.

I remembered the house. I remembered because I ran inside and stuck out my tongue to show Mom the tiny heart of my jawbreaker. It was a huge white house with four gables on the roof and columns on the porch. In the front yard—on a metal pole—stood a birdhouse that looked exactly the same as the big house.

It had to be somewhere nearby, and all of that would be proven true as soon as we got to Sandy's.

But Angelo was right. There was no store around the corner, just a vacant lot overgrown with prickly bushes. Styrofoam cups and McDonald's bags had blown in among the branches, and a huge wad of newspaper flyers lay rotting in the dirt.

"You want to go in and buy something?" asked Angelo.

"Maybe it was torn down," I said.

"Shut up. It was never here."

"He's right," said Zoe.

I felt confused. Angelo and Zoe had spent their whole lives near Deadman's Castle, and if they said there had never been a store they had to be right. But my memories were so clear. I'd looked out the window of that big white house and seen those ruins in the distance. I'd walked there with my dad, on a winter day when the snow was fresh and thick. He had pulled a cardboard box from a dumpster behind a flower store, and I'd used it for a sled on the hill below Deadman's Castle. I'd climbed into that box and gone rocketing down a path between the trees. There were broken flower stems inside, and red petals, and they'd flown up around me when I went over a jump at the bottom. Then I'd coasted across a big, flat field with Dad running behind me, laughing.

Those were all things I remembered. But if I was wrong about Sandy's, was I wrong about everything?

We spread out across the road, Zoe walking right along the yellow line, Angelo and Smasher on her left, me on her right. We passed a house that Angelo said was haunted, and while Zoe was laughing at him we came to the school where I'd gone to kindergarten.

I didn't say anything to Angelo or Zoe, but I was sure I was right. As we walked along the side of the building, I saw a red door that I remembered. Then we came to a playing field that backed onto the tree-covered hill, and I saw the path where I'd sledded in the flower box. The jump at the bottom was just a little cliff only two feet high. But it was still a cliff. In a hazy, dreamy way, everything made sense.

Except for Sandy's.

How could I remember a place that had never existed?

"WELCOME TO HELL"

We walked to the top of the hill in just a few minutes. I was disappointed to see that the ruins were just a few stubs of old brick walls that looked like they'd been smashed by a wrecking ball.

"Why do you call this Deadman's Castle?" I asked.

" 'Cause there's dead men in it," said Angelo. "There were bodies sealed up in the walls."

Zoe laughed.

"Well, that's what *I* heard," said Angelo, all defensive.

"It's just a dumb name," said Zoe.

"Why's it here?" I asked.

"The army built it," said Angelo. "To store bombs and stuff."

"Wrong," said Zoe.

Angelo was getting annoyed. "So who do *you* think built it?"

"A crazy old billionaire," said Zoe. "He wanted everything hidden under the ground, so he put this thing on top like a fort and dug out all these rooms and tunnels underneath."

"Why?" I asked.

Zoe shrugged with her hands in her pockets. "It was like a hundred years ago. I guess he was paranoid."

I found it hard to believe that a billionaire would build

a mansion inside a hill. But it was possible, and Zoe seemed to think it was true.

"There's all sorts of stairs and little rooms," she said. "It's pretty cool. You want to see?"

"Shouldn't we have a flashlight?" asked Angelo.

"Why? You don't need one," said Zoe.

"It's dark in there."

"Oh, don't be a baby. Come on."

Zoe stepped through a broken arch, down a shallow slope where the ground had washed into the ruins. Angelo followed her. "Stay close, Smashy," he said, though he didn't have to do that. She was only about two inches behind him.

We skidded down dirt and pebbles to the hard cement floor of Deadman's Castle. There was a sudden change from sunlight to gloom, from warmth to cold. If I'd been alone, I would have turned around and gone back.

The walls were covered with spray-painted messages about Satan, with devil faces and the number 666 dripping down the bricks. They faded into distant darkness where anything—or anyone—could have been hiding.

"It's too dark down here," said Angelo.

"It gets brighter in a bit," said Zoe. "Haven't you ever been in here before?"

"Lots of times. I just haven't gone this far into it."

"Then you'd better pick up your dog."

"Why?" asked Angelo.

"Just pick her up. You'll see."

Zoe started walking again, and I watched her black hair and black clothes vanish into the darkness. Angelo went behind her with Smasher panting in his arms, and he disappeared as well. It would have been too embarrassing to say I was afraid, so I followed them into the darkness.

I said, "Angelo, where are you?"

"Right here."

We both reached out, and our hands touched in the dark. Though he was standing almost right beside me, I couldn't see him.

Zoe moved through the blackness like a bat, while Angelo and I kept bumping into each other. Every now and then Smasher let out a frightened whimper.

"This is crazy," said Angelo. "I can't see nothin'."

"Just wait," said Zoe.

A patch of gray soon appeared. It became a doorway, and we walked into a room where a ray of sunlight beamed through a crack in the ceiling.

I smelled cigarette smoke. A putrid mattress lay in one corner, pulled halfway up against the wall to be both a chair and a bed. Wine bottles stood around it like fence posts, some stuffed full of cigarette butts, some with candle stubs wedged in their mouths. Scary messages were written on the walls: *Welcome to Hell. This is your future. Leave while you can.*

"Someone lives here sometimes," said Zoe. "The moon shines through that hole. So even at night it's not really dark in this room."

"You come here at *night?*" I asked.

"Sure. Why not?"

"I don't know about this," said Angelo. "I think Smasher wants to go back."

Zoe laughed. It was a strange sound in that place, like no one had ever laughed there before. She said, "You gotta go a bit farther. There's something really cool." Then she took a couple of steps and vanished again. We heard her boots going *clunk, clunk* down a corridor.

When they stopped, I had no idea where Zoe had gone. "Where are you?" I said, and my voice echoed from the walls.

There was a click, a spark, and a little flame appeared. A white skull hovered in the air. It was Zoe looking back, waiting for us in the corridor.

She kept the lighter burning till we reached her. In its yellow light her jewelry glittered like a cluster of stars, and Smasher's eyes were shining beads peering from Angelo's arms. On the floor by Zoe's feet lay two slim planks that seemed to warp and shift as she raised the lighter.

I stepped closer.

"Whoa!" shouted Zoe. Her hand emerged from the dark, reaching out to stop me.

There was no floor below the planks. They made a narrow bridge over a ten-foot-wide chasm so deep that it swallowed the light from Zoe's flame.

It might have been an empty stairway with the stairs taken out. Or an elevator shaft without the elevator. But to me it seemed like a bottomless pit, and there was no way to go around it. I thought we'd gone as far into Deadman's Castle as we could possibly go. But to Zoe it was nothing.

"We have to cross one at a time," she said. "Make sure you stay right in the middle or the planks will tip over."

I heard Angelo muttering to himself. I remembered how

he had been afraid of the swinging bridge—even in bright sunshine—and I knew the thought of crossing those planks must have terrified him even more than it terrified me. But, being Angelo, he would do it anyway. So I said, "You know, I've gone far enough."

"Okay, let's go back then," said Angelo.

"Wait," said Zoe. "Throw something down there."

"Like what?" I said.

"Hang on a sec."

The flame went out. Zoe's boots pattered away into the darkness. Afraid I might stumble into the pit, I got down on all fours and crawled to the edge. A hand touched my ankle, and Angelo crept up beside me.

A cold wind blowing up from the terrible darkness carried the eeriest sound I'd ever heard. It was like someone moaning, someone sighing, someone scratching at the floor. I whispered to Angelo, "Do you hear that?"

"No."

I didn't believe him. He answered too quickly, not even asking what I *thought* I'd heard. Beside me, he moved back from the edge.

When Zoe brought her little flame, it made our shadows enormous on the walls. She handed me a bottle, one of the empties from the room we'd passed through. "Drop it down there," she said.

I held the bottle over the hole and let it fall. For a second we could see it shining in the dark, a little speck shrinking quickly. Then it was gone, and we waited for the smash at the bottom. And we waited. And we waited.

I had time to think of what a nightmare it would be to fall down there, cartwheeling through the darkness. Then we heard a tiny smash as the bottle finally shattered.

"That's gotta be a *thousand feet!*" I said.

Zoe snorted. "Not even close. It's like only five stories."

She had to be right, but it didn't make any difference. If we fell into that hole, we would die.

• • •

We went back outside and sat in the sunshine. Angelo threw pebbles into the forest, and Smasher ran back and forth to chase them.

"I heard a kid died down there in the castle," Angelo said. "People could hear him screaming in the night. But it was two weeks before anyone found him."

"In four different rooms," added Zoe. "That's what *I* heard."

"Me too," said Angelo, nodding. "The kid was torn apart."

"By dogs?" I asked.

"By witches," said Zoe.

I didn't believe *that*. "Yeah, sure."

"Well, people who *call* themselves witches," she said. "They meet three stories down. They light candles and call up the devil."

"Have you seen them?" I asked.

"No, but I've *heard* them," said Zoe. "I've seen their circles on the floor. Their sacrifices."

"Like what?"

"You don't want to know," she said. "I wish *I'd* never seen it."

. . .

Angelo and I walked back to my house so he could get his sleeping bag. After he left, I decided to ask my mom about Sandy's. She was making her telemarketing calls in the kitchen and Bumble was coloring at the table.

"Hey, Mom," I said. "Do you remember a store called Sandy's?"

With a frown, she repeated the name. "Sandy's?"

"A little corner store somewhere. There was an old lady who sold candy."

"Oh, I don't know. It sounds familiar."

"Where was it?"

"I really don't remember. There have been so many places. Maybe you should ask your father."

"Yeah, right," I said.

"Well, I don't see why he shouldn't tell you."

Mom dialed someone's number and I thought she would forget all about Sandy's. But when Dad came home in his clown suit, carrying his big shoes hooked on his fingers, it was the first thing she mentioned. "Igor was asking about a place called Sandy's," she said. "Do you remember it?"

He turned to look at me. "Now why are you thinking of Sandy's?"

Through his clown makeup, I couldn't tell if he was angry or curious, so I just shrugged and gave him my standard answer. "I dunno."

"Sandy's was the little store around the corner from where I grew up. I've told you about it. How I thought the old woman who ran it was a witch. How the door used to swing shut like a mousetrap."

"I never went there?" I asked.

"Of course not. You've never been within a thousand miles of Sandy's." Dad was smiling at his memories. "It's funny those stories made such an impression on you. Remember what I used to buy there?"

"Jawbreakers?" I asked.

"No," he said. "You were the one who liked jawbreakers. I got Popsicles at Sandy's. Root beer Popsicles."

"Yuck!" cried Bumble with her tongue sticking out.

That made everyone laugh. Except for me.

So my memory was real, but it wasn't mine. I had stolen it from my dad and mixed it in with my own, and that made me wonder what else I'd gotten wrong. My memories were like the tombstones in the cemetery, chipped and broken, so jumbled around that they didn't make sense. Maybe I was trying to connect things that couldn't be connected.

THE OLD HOUSE

Angelo could hardly wait for the end of school and the start of summer vacation. He thought the days were oozing along at slug speed. But for me they were flying past. I loved going to Rutherford B. Hayes, and I wished school would never end.

It was the last Monday in May when I woke up to a thunderstorm. I heard our quiet little river now roaring along, surging past the house. It had risen by three or four inches overnight, and rain was still falling. The only coat I had was the one I'd worn all winter, so I put it on and slogged to school.

As I waited for Angelo at Mr. Meanie's fence, the storm ended with explosions of sunlight and birdsong. Angelo arrived in a yellow raincoat, as dry as a bone underneath it. But I walked into school like a human sponge, dripping water down the hall. Zoe told me, "You need new clothes."

"I'll ask my mom for money," I said.

"No, this is an emergency," said Zoe. "You need them today."

"But I can't—"

"Don't worry about it," she said. "I help out in the store sometimes. I get credit. You can pay me back later."

We left right after school, and I didn't even *think* about crossing Jefferson until I was already on the other side. With a pang of guilt I remembered what my father had said. *We can't afford to become complacent.*

From a block away, I could see him in his clown suit. So I told Zoe, "Let's go this way," and we turned north on the street before Dead End Road. At the Salvation Army, Zoe's mom sat in the same place. She said hello like we were old friends.

Zoe bustled up and down the racks picking out clothes. "Try these on," she told me. "I'll browse."

She left me with a pile of rain jackets and summer things. There were shorts and baseball caps and Hawaiian shirts that I didn't really like because they made my arms look as thin as spaghetti. Every time I came out of the changing booth to ask "What do you think?" Zoe was in a different place. She sorted through the jeans and dresses, through the jigsaw puzzles and the knickknacks.

When I stepped out in a pair of brown shorts and a yellow shirt, she glanced at me. "You look SpongeBob SquarePants," she said. "Now come and see what I found."

I went back to the changing booth and put on my old clothes. When I came out I found Zoe sitting on the floor, looking through a shelf of old books.

"What are those?" I asked.

"City directories," she said. "You look up an address and you can see who used to live there. It's like time traveling."

She pulled out a book as big as a cinder block. A sparkling cloud of dust rose from the pages as she flipped through them. "This is like forty years ago," she said. "Most of these people are dead. Everything's changed, but in the book it stays the same forever."

. . .

I left the store with a huge bag of clothes hanging over my shoulder. The only thing Zoe got for herself was a tiny silver crucifix.

We took a back alley from the Salvation Army, walking past garages and garbage cans. I told Zoe, "She's nice. Your mom."

"Yeah, she is," said Zoe.

"You don't look like her."

"Why should I?" she said. "I'm adopted."

"Huh." So at least part of Trevis's story was true.

I thought that was probably all I'd ever learn about Zoe. She didn't offer anything else, and suddenly she was gone. Without a word, she'd stopped and let me go on without her. When I looked back, she was opening a gate made of wood and wire.

"What are you doing?" I asked.

"Going home," she said. "This is where I live."

From the back, the house was a lot like Angelo's, small and cozy-looking. I thought it was far too ordinary to be a home for Zoe.

"You want to come inside?" she asked.

I said, "Sure."

She kept the key under a flowerpot on the back porch. I imagined Dad passing out if he saw something like that, but I wished I could live as free from fear as Zoe.

Her house was stuffed with things that must have come from the Salvation Army. There were racks of tiny spoons, shelves full of old teacups. I counted six clocks just on the way to Zoe's room.

Three teddy bears and a little unicorn lay on her bed. For a table she used an old trunk plastered with faded labels. TWA. IMPERIAL LODGE. GRAND HOTEL. There were so many that they overlapped each other. That trunk must have gone around the world a dozen times.

Zoe took away the things she kept on top—a book, a lamp, a box full of rings and bracelets—and moved them neatly to the floor. Then she crouched beside the trunk to open the latches.

"I've never shown this to anyone," she said. "Don't laugh at me, okay?"

The latches were made of brass that had rusted around the edges. They snapped open with hollow thunking sounds. I leaned forward as Zoe raised the lid.

I didn't know what to expect. Tombstone rubbings? A collection of coffin nails? Vampire capes and wooden crosses? I didn't think anything would surprise me, but I was wrong.

The trunk was mostly empty. There was a little stack of magazines and a few newspapers wrapped in plastic. Zoe smiled. "They're all about Kate," she told me.

"Who's Kate?" I asked.

"Who's *Kate*? Only Her Royal Highness the Duchess of Cambridge. Only the future Queen of England."

I had hurt Zoe's feelings by not knowing that. I looked over her shoulder at magazines with titles like *The Royal*

Baby and *The Royal Wedding,* and I had no idea what to say. There was something sad about the collection, the way Zoe kept it so carefully and perfectly arranged. It made me feel embarrassed, like I'd seen her undressing or something.

"I guess I shouldn't have shown you," said Zoe. She closed the trunk but stayed bent over it. "Could you go away, please? I'll see you tomorrow at school."

Her hair fell on each side of her neck. I could see her pale skin underneath.

I didn't say goodbye. I took my bag of clothes and headed home. But without Zoe to guide me, I didn't know the way, and I found myself wandering down strange streets without a clue where I was. Purely by accident, I found the house where I'd lived before.

Like Deadman's Castle and the hill behind the school, it wasn't exactly the way I remembered. There were only two gables. The lawn was tiny. My memories had made everything bigger and grander—except the birdhouse. Instead of the tiny replica I remembered, it was a big, clunky thing that sat crooked on its post.

A funny feeling ran through me as I stared at the old house. I had walked through that front door. Mom had grown flowers in those window boxes. Dad had pushed a mower back and forth across that lawn. In my mind I could hear its thrumming roar again, and I could smell the fresh-cut grass. There was no doubt in my mind that a policeman the size of a grizzly bear had squeezed through that front door and sat all night in the kitchen.

Someone else was living there now. I could see an old

man peering down at me from an upstairs window, probably wondering what I was doing outside *his* house.

I wondered if Dad had made his rules to keep me from finding out that we'd lived here before, and if that was why Mom had acted so strangely in the Buena Vista, and especially on the day we'd first come to Dead End Road. But why would the Protectors send us back to where it all began? It didn't make sense.

And where was the Lizard Man?

FLOWER BOXES

On Saturday I stuffed my toothbrush in my pocket and walked over to Angelo's house for our sleepover. But he wasn't home.

"Angelo's gone out," Mrs. Bonito told me at the door. "He took his big glove. For baseball. He said for you to meet him at the park."

When I got there, Angelo and another boy were choosing teams. Kids had lined up on each side of the backstop, and Smasher was asleep behind home plate, curled in a little hole she had dug in the dust.

"We'll take Igor," said Angelo when I was the only one left. I was *always* the last to be chosen, the only kid who ever did bat flips by mistake.

I was banished to the wilderness of far left field, where I stood around hoping the ball would never reach me. When I went to bat, someone shouted, "Move in!" and the outfielders came jogging all the way past second base. The pitcher threw easy lobs that were hard to miss. But somehow I managed.

After a couple of innings I was ready to quit. But the others said, "C'mon, Igor. Don't give up now." I figured they wanted me to play for comic relief, but at least I was part of the team.

. . .

Mrs. Bonito made pancakes for breakfast on Sunday morning.
She piled them into big stacks, like tires in a wrecker's yard,
and covered them with butter and maple syrup. I ate ten of
them, and Angelo ate even more.

"So what do you want to do?" he asked when we finished.

"I don't know," I said. "What do you want to do?"

"We could go to Deadman's Castle. You can see Smasher
do her bloodhound thing."

I didn't think Dad would be working that day, so I didn't
worry too much about crossing Jefferson. I just hunched down
and watched for the jelly bean car. Then, safe on the other
side, I steered Angelo up and down the side streets until we
passed the house where I'd lived before.

"See that place?" I asked. "I think I used to live there."

He grunted.

"I remember—"

"You don't remember anything." Angelo scowled. "Now
quit it, Watson. I'm not kidding. This isn't funny."

We crossed the swinging bridge in silence, but instead
of heading straight for Deadman's Castle we turned to walk
beside the river. Once again it was Smasher's decision. Angelo
had put the leash in his pocket so we just followed her.

She stopped to sniff at every telephone pole, at every
tree and fence, then dashed along to the next one. We passed
behind a row of businesses. There was a dentist's office and a
drugstore, then a building that looked like a church. Beside a
wire fence, a green dumpster overflowed with cardboard
boxes.

As soon as I saw them, I knew they were flower boxes. I remembered their waxy touch, their particular smell of roses and lilies. Even from the street I could see petals and dried-out stems scattered around the dumpster.

But it wasn't a flower store.

The building had narrow windows made of stained glass, and double doors wide enough to fit a hearse. My father had raided the garbage of a funeral home. He'd sent me sledding in a box meant to carry flowers for dead people.

That seemed a little creepy, and I wasn't sure how I felt to see that another memory, though broken, was basically true. I wanted to talk to Angelo about it, to figure out what it all meant. But I was afraid of starting an argument that would make us mad at each other, so I didn't say a thing.

Step by step we marched along, and soon we were back on the roads we'd taken the first time we'd gone to Deadman's Castle. We reached the school, then crossed the field behind it and started up the hill.

When we got to the ruins at the summit, Angelo clipped Smasher's leash to her collar. "Hold her here," he told me. "I'll go into the castle and she can do her bloodhound thing."

I didn't expect very much as Angelo went scurrying down to hide in the castle. I counted to a hundred, then took off Smasher's leash and told her, "Go find Angelo!"

She went off like a shot—in the wrong direction. I had to catch her and lead her back, right into the entrance. I saw Angelo crouched like a gnome just inside the doorway.

But Smasher still couldn't find him.

He started whispering, "Smashy!" She wandered right past his feet, nosing in the dust.

"Great bloodhound," I said.

"Try again," said Angelo. He made me try seven times in all, but Smasher never found him once. "It's 'cause she knows I'm not lost," he said. "If I was *really* in trouble, she wouldn't be fooling around."

"Yeah, sure," I said, thinking he was joking.

But he got angry. "It's true. She'd find me then, all right. She's a tracking dog."

We went down the hill in silence, walking farther apart than we'd ever walked before. It made me feel sick to think that I was losing my friend. I couldn't bear to let that happen.

I said, "Angelo, I gotta tell you something."

THE BOOGEYMAN

At the river we stopped to sit for a while beside the swinging bridge.

It hung higher than ever above the water. There had been no rain since the thunderstorm, and the summertime heat had turned the wintertime river into something more like a creek. It was so shallow that I could see all sorts of stuff lying on the bottom, things people had tossed from the bridge. There were pennies and soda cans, and a tricycle covered in weeds that were waving back and forth in the current.

Angelo held Smasher close in front of him and waited for me to talk.

"When I was a little kid," I told him, "my dad saw someone do a bad thing."

"Like what?" asked Angelo.

"I don't know," I said. "He never told me. But he went to the police, and ever since then there's been a guy coming after us."

"Like the Terminator?"

"Not exactly," I said. "But something like that. Everywhere we go, he comes after us."

"Why? What's he's going to do?"

"Who knows?" I said. "He told my dad, 'I'm going to get even.'"

Angelo looked down at the river. "Wow," he said softly.

"It started when I was a little kid," I said. "A policeman came and sat in our kitchen with a rifle. I remember my mom was scared; she cried a lot. Then one day we left the house and never went back. We moved away, and we've been moving ever since. Everywhere we go, we start over. We change our names and everything."

"Huh," said Angelo. "So what moron named you Igor?"

I didn't answer that. But I told him everything else, all about the Protectors and Dad's rules and bugging out in the middle of the night. I spilled all the secrets I'd kept for years. I'd always had a strange idea that telling them would make something awful happen, and even with Angelo there beside me I kept looking up and down the river. I half expected to see the Lizard Man slithering out of the water.

"We've moved so many times I can't remember all the places," I said. "I can't even remember my real name. But I'm sure this is where it started. In that house I showed you."

Angelo plucked a blade of grass and twirled it in his fingers. I didn't know what he was thinking, and I waited for him to speak. Finally, he shook his head and told me, "It doesn't make sense. Why would your dad go back to where everything started?"

"He didn't have a choice," I said. "We have to go where the Protectors send us."

"To the Terminator's hometown? No way they'd send you there." Angelo tried to hurl the grass stem toward the river, but it fluttered down beside his foot. "Think about it,

Watson. Why do you close your curtains and lock the doors and go in and out like it's maximum security?"

"Because there's a crazy guy out there."

"The only crazy guy out there lives in your house," said Angelo.

"But it's true," I said. "I don't know why we've been here so long. Maybe the guy quit looking for us. Maybe he died and no one knows it. Or he might find us tomorrow."

"What's his name?"

"I call him the Lizard Man."

Angelo laughed. "Watson, you're as loony as your dad."

That made me angry. I said, "He's got a lizard tattoo, okay? It's scary, Angelo."

"Why?"

" 'Cause wherever we go, he follows us."

"How do you know that?" asked Angelo. "Have you seen him?"

"No, but Dad—"

"Have you *heard* him?"

"No, but Dad—"

"Yeah, it's always your dad, right?" Angelo shook his head. "You're such a loser."

"Why?"

"There's no Lizard Man."

I stared at Angelo; he stared right back. He pulled up another blade of grass and said, "Your dad made him up to scare you. He's just your bogeyman."

"Bogeyman?" I said.

"Whatever. Every parent invents a bogeyman. My mom called him Babau." Angelo did a perfect imitation of his mother. *"Holy smackerels, Babau will get you. I was scared to death."*

I tried to imagine a tiny Angelo afraid of the boogeyman.

"But Babau never got me," he said. "So my mom started throwing in other stuff to scare me. Watch out for this; watch out for that."

She sounded just like Dad with his big cars and black cars and his men in dark glasses. But there was one difference between them. "My dad's afraid too," I said. "He's not pretending."

"I know it," said Angelo. "Your dad's been running around saying that stuff so long that he actually believes it. He's a psycho, Watson. Your dad's a nutbar."

"What about the policeman in the kitchen?"

"You dreamed him up."

"The Protectors?"

"You ever seen them? Ever talked to them?"

"Mom's tears?"

"If I was married to your dad, *I'd* be crying."

He had an explanation for everything. But I thought there was one question he could never answer. "So why did my dad come back?"

"Who knows? He liked the neighborhood." Angelo twirled his finger around Smasher's ear. "Why don't you just ask him?"

"He'd only get mad," I said. "He never tells me anything."

But what if Angelo was right, and all the years we'd spent

running from place to place had been wasted? Could my dad really have made up the Lizard Man and the Protectors?

"Hey, Watson," said Angelo.

"What?"

"Maybe we knew each other in kindergarten."

"Did you go to the school by Deadman's Castle?"

"Yeah"

"Then maybe we did."

THE SKINNY MAN

Another week flew by and suddenly it was Friday. A girl named Hayden announced that she was planning a year-end party at her house. It would be on the last day of school, only two weeks away.

Hayden was tall and pretty, and she always chewed bubble gum that smelled like watermelon. I didn't know her very well, but it made me feel special that she gave me an invitation, along with everybody else.

I tried to imagine what a party might be like. I thought about it over and over: music playing loudly, everybody crowded together. Sometimes I saw myself laughing and having fun, girls coming up one after the other to ask me to dance. But other times I was sure I'd end up standing alone against the wall, ignored by everybody.

Zoe told me I *had* to go. "It's going to be epic," she said. "You gotta get new clothes."

"When?" I asked.

"Can you go today?"

"Sure."

"Then go," said Zoe. "Right after school. Use my credit."

"You're not going with me?" I asked.

"I'm not your mother," she said. "I can't dress you *all* the time."

I'd never crossed Jefferson by myself. I got a bit lost and

ended up passing the house where I'd lived before. Seeing it gave me an idea, the sort of thing that would make Dad absolutely furious if he knew what I was up to. But I couldn't imagine how it could do any harm, so I opened my backpack and took out a pen. On a scrap of paper ripped from a notebook, I wrote down the address and hurried along to the Salvation Army.

Zoe's mother wasn't there. On the stool behind the counter sat a man with a bushy white beard that made him look like a garden gnome. He said, "May I help you?"

"Just looking," I told him, hoping Zoe's mom would show up very soon.

"Looking is free," he said. "But if you break it you buy it."

As I walked through the store he watched me all the time, leaning this way and that, stretching his neck. When he couldn't see me anymore he followed me down the aisles, tidying things that didn't need to be tidied.

I chose a pair of jeans and a nice shirt, then went straight to the directories that Zoe had shown me. They were arranged by year, going back nearly half a century. As the bearded man watched me, pretending that he wasn't, I pulled out the volume for the year I'd started kindergarten.

It stank of old attics and damp basements, a smell that tickled my nose and made the gnome sneeze.

I could hear him muttering to himself. He sneezed again and wiped his nose with his fingers. In a louder voice he snapped at me. "Do you intend to buy that book?"

"Can't I just look?" I asked.

"It's not a library."

The gnome retreated to his place behind the cash register, then rearranged things on the counter to give himself a clear view of me and the books. I found the right address and, beside it, a name that didn't sound familiar. But I hoped it was mine. I got out my pen and piece of paper and wrote it down, though there wasn't a chance I'd ever forget that name. I wanted to turn it into something I could see and hold. To make it real.

I left without the jeans and shirt. The bearded man refused to let me take them on Zoe's credit. So I walked out with nothing more than the piece of paper. I held it clenched in my fist, and that night I lay in bed reading the name over and over until I fell asleep.

· · ·

The next day, Angelo and I hung out at the park on Dead End Road. We sat beside the river and threw sticks into the shrunken stream, racing them over the shallows. Mine kept snagging in the weeds, and I soon got tired of it.

I rolled over on my stomach and picked through a patch of clover, looking for one with four leaves. I said, "You know that house across Jefferson?"

"You mean where you lived when you were little?" asked Angelo.

"Yeah." I ran my fingers through the tiny plants. "I looked it up in a directory at the Salvation Army. I found out who lived there."

"Who?"

I sat up again and hauled the piece of paper from my pocket. By then it was scrunched and dirty, and Angelo frowned as I unfolded it carefully. He snatched it away and looked at the name. *Robert Weaver.*

"So you think this is your dad?" he asked.

"Yeah," I said.

He grunted. "It's possible."

"You really think so?"

"You *look* like a Weaver."

He turned the paper over and saw the other names I'd written on the back. "What's this?" he asked.

"I was trying to remember my first name," I said.

He read them aloud. "Thor? Kodiak? Rocky?" Then he laughed. "I don't see you as a Rocky."

"Then what do *you* think?" I asked.

"Percy," he said. "No. Willy. I bet you were Wee Willy Weaver."

I snatched the scrap of paper and shoved it into my pocket.

Angelo snapped a stick in two and threw half of it into the river. "You going to show that to your dad?" he asked.

"No way." I threw the other half of the stick beside his. "But I was thinking...What if you go up to my mom and say, 'Hello, Mrs. Weaver.' See what she does."

"That's the dumbest idea I ever heard," said Angelo.

"Maybe *I'll* try it," I said. Then my stick ran aground, and Angelo said, "Let's do something else."

AN INNOCENT CHICKEN

Angelo's uncle Paolo died and his mother had to fly to Toronto for the funeral. He came home with me the next Friday, planning to stay two nights.

Mom said, "I'm sorry your uncle died." But Angelo only shrugged and said, "I don't even know him. He calls at Christmas and talks to Ma in Italian. He forgets my name."

That Saturday was kind of gray and miserable. Angelo and I didn't feel like going out, so we just lay around in the living room after breakfast, watching one of Bumble's DVDs with her and Hideous George.

Dad came in with his second cup of coffee. "So how do you boys plan to spend the day?" he asked.

"I don't know," I said. "There's nothing to do around here."

"Nothing to do?" He was trying to act like we were all best friends, the Three Amigos. "Well, what would you be doing if you were at Angelo's house?"

"Playing video games," I told him.

"Oh."

It wasn't like he was mad at me for that. He sounded more disappointed.

"You could read books," he said.

"Yeah, Dad, thanks," I said.

You can only watch so much of *Thomas the Tank Engine* before you feel kind of sick. Especially if you've seen it a dozen times before. So Angelo and I went out and messed around till the middle of the afternoon.

When we got back to my room we found a box placed on my bed. *Alfred Chicken,* it said in big yellow letters. Inside was a gaming system that thrilled me at first, until I saw what it was: an ancient Game Boy with a screen the size of a Post-it note.

Angelo laughed when he saw it. "Where do you think your dad found that?" he asked.

I shrugged. "At Fun and Games, I guess." It might have been sitting on a shelf for years, unopened.

Angelo read the blurbs on the box as I put in the batteries and plugged in the game. "'An innocent chicken. In a startling world,'" he said. "Hey, it has sound effects."

The screen was gray and black. I took one look and tossed the thing back on the bed. "Thanks for nothing, Dad," I said.

"Hey, c'mon," said Angelo. "Let's try it out."

"Why? You wanna be an innocent chicken in a startling world?"

"Not really," he said. "But your dad went out and bought that to make you happy."

"Or to spy on me with it."

"See? You're as crazy as he is." Angelo dropped the empty box on my bed. "Start it up."

The game had different levels, but every one was pretty much the same. You had to peck balloons and gather diamonds as you tried to get a pot of jam from Mr. Peckles. There was

hideous music and sound effects that never changed. *Beep.*
Beep. Beep.

For an hour we passed the machine back and forth. Then
Dad knocked on the door and came in.

I thought he'd be angry to find Smasher on the bed. But
he barely glanced toward her. As soon as he saw us playing
the game his face lit up. "Do you like it?" he asked.

"Yes, Dad." And I actually meant it. "Thanks."

His smile blurred into his old look of worry. "I wasn't
sure if it was the right choice," he said. "I don't know much
about video games."

"You wanna try, Mr. Watson?" asked Angelo.

"Yeah, Dad." I held the Game Boy toward him.

Back came the smile. "Thank you, but no," Dad said. "I
came up to say we're going out, your mother and I. We've
decided to see a movie at the Bijou. Is that okay?"

"Sure," I said.

"We might not be back before dark."

I knew what *that* meant. "So Amy's coming over," I said.

"No, no." Dad held up his hands like he was stopping
traffic. "It's only two hours. Your mother thinks you boys
will be fine on your own. I just wanted to ask if you'll look
after Bumble."

"Sure," I said.

"You'll keep her in sight at all times?"

"Yes, Dad."

He left, and as soon as the door clicked shut behind him,
Angelo asked, "Who's Amy?"

"Never mind," I told him.

But he'd already guessed. "She's your babysitter, isn't she?"

"Shut up, Bonito."

He laughed. "I bet your folks get a sitter every time they go out."

"They never go out," I told him.

"*Never?* Come on."

"Well, almost," I said.

"You know why they didn't call a sitter?"

" 'Cause *you're* here?" I imagined we were thinking the same thing, that Angelo would be my sitter. But he shook his head.

"No," he told me. "It's because they're not really going anywhere. They'll drive a little way down the street, then stop and watch the house."

"Why?"

"To test you."

"We're looking after Bumble," I said. "Where are we going to go?"

"We could take her down to the river. Out to the park," said Angelo, waving his hands in each direction. "It doesn't matter. They want to see if you open the curtains or something. It's a test, Watson. Maybe they'll knock on the door and see if you open it without asking who's there."

"I don't know," I said. "Dad might do something like that. But not Mom."

Angelo had to think for a while. I could imagine little gears whirring in his head, calculating an answer. "I know," he said when it came to him. "Your dad will find a reason to leave your mom alone at the movies. Then he'll come back and watch the house."

An hour later, after an early supper, we were all standing at the door. Even Smasher was there, wagging her tiny tail. But Bumble clung to Mom's legs and pleaded with her not to leave. Mom kept saying, "Bumblebee, please," and "Sweetie, it's all right," until Dad finally pulled them apart and got Mom into the minivan. Poor Bumble stood crying as Dad backed down the driveway.

He made it almost to the street before he stopped. His window opened; he leaned out and yelled at us. "Go back inside now. Make sure the doors are locked. Keep the curtains drawn."

I gave him a wave to show that I'd heard; then we sealed ourselves into the house. I put the chain on its slider; I threw the dead bolt, and Bumble wept beside me, holding tightly to her grumpy.

There was only one way to cheer her up that never failed. I said, "Who wants ice cream?"

"Sure!" said Angelo.

Mom's telemarketing stuff was still spread out on the kitchen table, so I pushed it into a pile and stacked the spy phone on top. Angelo sat on one side, Bumble on the other, and I opened the freezer to get the ice cream. Smasher stood right at my feet, staring up, shuffling sideways to keep from being stepped on.

Behind me, Bumble said, "You better not do that," and I looked around to see Angelo fiddling with the phone. I said, "Yeah, don't do that. It's my mom's."

"I'm not going to hurt it," said Angelo. He put on the headset. "Is this that phone that doesn't have a number?"

I'd forgotten that I'd told him that, why I couldn't call my folks from his house. "Yes," I said.

"It can't be traced?"

"No," I said. "Why?"

His fingers hovered over the buttons. "You ever make prank calls?"

I'd never even *thought* of doing that. The spy phone was something never to be touched.

Angelo turned to my sister. "Hey, Bumble," he said. "You want to watch a video while you eat your ice cream?"

"I'm not allowed," said Bumble.

"Oh, this one time will be all right," he said. "Don't you think so, Igor?"

It was obvious that he wanted her out of the room. I didn't know why, but I went along with it and got Bumble settled in front of the TV with a little bowl of ice cream and a Pokémon video. Smasher lay right in front of her, and they started sharing the ice scream spoon for spoon.

The Pokémon shrieked, and my sister giggled, and I went back to the kitchen.

Angelo said, "Take off your sock."

I said, "What?"

"I want to call that phone number."

This did not seem to me like a good idea. "No," I said.

"Why not?" said Angelo. "No one's going to know."

"But—"

"Relax, Watson. What do you think's going to happen?"

I had no answer for that. In all the years I had carried the number around I had never thought of calling it.

"It's probably some stupid number to a phone booth somewhere," said Angelo.

When I didn't do what he wanted, Angelo got mad. His eyes went to slits; his voice hardened. "Are you scared?"

"No," I said.

"Then let's do it."

I felt like I had no choice. I took off my sock, pulled out the money. Angelo dialed the number.

Through the tiny speaker in the headset came the ringing of a telephone. I pictured black helicopters suddenly thrumming overhead, Navy Seals sliding down ropes, men in body armor bursting through the door with machine guns.

Ring.

A man answered right away, his voice deep and growly. He said, "Talk to me."

I stared at Angelo; he stared at me. Then he pressed the button to end the call and dropped the headset. He even unplugged the phone from the wall, yanking hard on the cord. "Who *was* that?" he said.

It was the creepiest thing I'd ever heard.

WHAT HAPPENS WHEN YOU TELL A SECRET

There was no way we were going to sit and watch Pokémon with Bumble. So we dragged her up to my room and played *Alfred Chicken* as she rolled on the bed with Smasher. We pecked the stupid balloons and tried not to think about our phone call.

My room was unbearably hot. But Angelo had made the window slide so easily that it wouldn't stay open on its own. So I propped it up with one of my schoolbooks and the cardboard box from *Alfred Chicken*. Bumble lay on my bed to look out at the backyard, through curtains that flapped open and shut in the warm breeze from the river. Outside, it was getting dark. But the room pulsed with the glow of the video screen.

It was my turn with the game when Bumble suddenly shouted, "Igor, look!"

"Wait a minute," I told her.

But she shrieked even louder. "There's someone across the river."

Angelo got onto the bed. He pulled the curtains aside and leaned on the windowsill. "Hey, she's right," he said. "There *is* someone out there."

My chicken bounced on a spring and flapped its stubby wings. It landed on a snail that was scuttling across the screen. *Beep-beep-beeeep.* My game ended.

Angelo was kneeling on the bed with his arms stretched across the window. Both Smasher and Bumble peered around him.

The sun had just set. On the far side of the river, a light was moving through the forest. It turned and bobbed, flared and faded, sometimes bursting into a sudden glare as it reflected off the water.

The Protectors, I thought. They were coming already. I said, "I knew we shouldn't have made that call."

Angelo laughed. "Calm down, Watson. It's your dad. I told you he'd watch the house."

It could have been anybody on the other side of the river. All I could see was the glare of the flashlight. But Angelo was so sure of himself that he waved his arms and yelled. "Hi, Mr. Watson!"

"Whoever that is, he's too far away to hear you," I said. "And he can't see you in the dark."

"So turn the light on."

"No," I said. "That's breaking the rules, Angelo."

"Forget the rules. It's a good joke." His voice had that edge to it again. "Bumble, turn on the light."

"Don't," I said. But she hopped off the bed and ran across the room. That got Smasher excited, and she bounded off the bed to chase Bumble.

I wasn't fast enough to stop her. She flicked the switch and the light glared from the ceiling, shining down on Angelo as he waved through the window.

"I think he saw me!" he said. "Look, he's going away now."

I shut off the light. Still standing in the blackened

window, Angelo was laughing. But the thought of Dad crawling through the forest made me cringe with embarrassment. I didn't want to see that. I told Angelo, "Close the curtains."

"Why?"

"If that's Dad he's going to be mad. He'll ground me again."

"No he won't," said Angelo. "He'd have to admit he was spying on you."

"Well, maybe," I said. "But don't say anything when he comes back. Okay?"

"Don't worry about *me.*" Angelo pointed a thumb toward Bumble.

She was sitting beside Smasher. I told her, "Listen, Bumble, let's not tell Dad we saw him."

"Is it a secret?" asked Bumble.

"Yes, it's a secret," I said.

My folks came back less than half an hour later. Dad gave his secret knock to let me know it was him. I opened the door.

Mom was so happy that she danced around the house while Dad locked and chained the door again. She grabbed Bumble by the hands and whirled her down the hall. "We saw the most wonderful movie," she said. "It was a love story."

"Did you like it, Dad?" I asked.

"Not so much."

I tried to guess his mood as he turned from the door and looked at me. I was afraid he'd be angry, but instead he seemed embarrassed.

"The ending got a bit sappy," said Mom. "So your father left early. He went out to sit in the car."

Angelo caught my eye and winked.

Dad went upstairs to change. He never said a word about the river, or what he might have seen.

• • •

I walked Angelo home on Sunday afternoon. We played video games till his mother arrived in a yellow taxi. I was only gone for three or four hours, but when I got back and tapped our secret knock on the door, it was Amy who let me in. I couldn't have been more surprised.

She stopped yakking on her cell phone just long enough to say, "Your sister's in the living room. Your mom'll be back soon." Then she gave the door a kick to swing it shut and started talking into the phone again.

"Where's Mom and Dad?" I asked.

Amy didn't answer. Without a break in her conversation, she threw the dead bolt and put the chain on the latch. Then she leaned back against the wall—still talking—and let herself slide down to the floor.

"What's going on?" I said.

She held the phone away from her ear. "Your mom took the car and went shopping. Your dad got called into work. Okay? Maybe there was some sort of clown emergency."

"Why didn't Mom take Bumble?"

"I don't know!" Amy sounded annoyed.

I went into the living room. Bumble was sitting on the couch, watching My Little Pony prance across the TV.

She had spread her grumpy across her lap, and Hideous

George was sitting on top of it. I shook his hand and said, "How do you do, Hideous?"

Bumble laughed. She looked up at me, all smiling and happy. "Guess what?"

"What?"

She looked around dramatically, then waved for me to put my head next to hers. Into my ear she whispered, "I saw him."

"Who?"

"You know." She made that grimacing little grin I liked so much, and she whispered again. "The Lizard Man."

A BLACK CAR

I tried not to look surprised. But I felt the way a football coach must feel to have an ice bucket suddenly emptied down his back. There was a terrible shock, and then a chill that went right through me.

We would bug out.

That was my first thought, and it was even more frightening than the Lizard Man. Before the sun went down, we'd probably be gone. Dad would cover my head with a blanket and cram me into the minivan, and off we'd go to somewhere else. A new house, a new name. A new life.

I wouldn't have a chance to say goodbye to Angelo or Zoe. Not to Mr. Little or Mr. Moran or anybody else at Rutherford B. Hayes. By the time school started in the morning I might be two hundred miles away, and I'd never see any of them again. For a while they would wonder what had happened, and then they'd forget all about me.

I couldn't bear to think of it. At that moment, I thought I would rather be dead.

My Little Pony whinnied and laughed. In the hall, Amy kept talking on her phone, so I grabbed Bumble's arm and pulled her toward me. "How do you know it was the Lizard Man?" I said. "What did you see?"

"You're hurting me," she said.

"Tell me what you saw!"

Her lip started quivering. In another moment she'd be crying, and that would bring Amy running. I told Bumble, "Let's go to the kitchen."

"I wanna watch *My Little Pony*," she said. Her legs were sticking straight out in front of her across the sofa cushion.

"I'll give you ice cream," I told her.

"No."

I snatched Hideous George from her lap. Bumble reached up, shrieking. "Give him back!"

Amy looked in through the doorway, her cell phone in her hand. "Could you kids keep it down?" she said. "I'm trying to have a conversation."

I tried pulling Bumble again, but she clung like a tick to the sofa. "Leave me alone!" she whined.

Leaning down, I whispered again. "I'll give you a cookie."

There was nothing Bumble wouldn't do for a cookie. In an instant she stopped yelling. "Okay," she said.

We left My Little Pony prancing away in the living room. I got Bumble sitting at the kitchen table, then took an Oreo from the cupboard and sat across from her.

"Are you *sure* you saw the Lizard Man?" I asked.

She nodded. Her eyes seemed fixed on the cookie.

"Where did you see him?"

"Out on the road."

"Why were you looking out the window? You're not supposed to do that."

Bumble made a little gasp. "Umm, I forgot," she said.

"It's okay. I won't tell Mom and Dad," I said. "Why did you look out the window?"

"I heard a car. It stopped outside," said Bumble. "I thought it was Mom, so I looked out and I saw him. He was sitting in his car, staring at the house."

"What sort of a car?"

"Black," she said. "I want my cookie."

"Just a minute." Every time I moved my hand, her head turned to follow it. "How did you know it was the Lizard Man? Did you see a lizard on his skin?"

Bumble pretended to think, a finger on her lip. "I don't remember."

"Yes you do." I held the cookie closer. "What did you see, Bumblebee?"

The little rhyme would usually make her laugh. But she only stared intently at the Oreo. "He looked funny," she said. "Like a lizard."

"How?"

"He had big eyes sticking out." She made circles with her fingers around her eyes. "He had a wrinkly face, and his neck was droopy." She pulled at her skin, stretching it down from her jaw. "He didn't have much hair."

She might have been describing any old man. When I was her age, I'd gone running in fear from every wrinkled coot who looked toward me. Bumble's Lizard Man was probably just a poor old grandpa with baggy skin and liver spots who got lost on our street.

But he *might* have been the Lizard Man.

I didn't know what to do. If I told Dad, he'd take me out of school and move us across the country. But if I didn't tell him, and he somehow found out, he would be so furious that he'd probably take me out of school anyway, and ground me for life as well.

Your dad's a nutbar. Angelo had told me that. In his mind, the Lizard Man wasn't even real. *He's just your boogeyman.*

Bumble shouted at me, "I want my cookie now!"

"Just a minute." I wasn't ready to give it to her. "Did you tell Amy what you saw?"

She shook her head violently. "Dad said not to tell anyone else."

I remembered him saying that when he'd given her the talk. *You can tell your mom, or tell your brother, whoever's closest. But don't tell anyone else.*

I held the cookie a little closer. "You know what? I think we should keep this a secret, don't you?"

"You mean the cookie?" asked Bumble.

"No, the old man," I said. "I don't think we should tell Mom or Dad about him."

"Why?"

"Because we'd have to move away. You don't want to do that, do you?"

"No," she said.

"You like living here. Don't you?"

She nodded, her head moving up and down while her eyes stayed locked on the cookie.

"Then it has to be a secret. Right?"

I let Bumble touch the Oreo. Then I pulled it back. Frustrated, she drummed her fists on the table and shouted, "Give me my cookie!"

"Okay." Again I slid it closer, but not so close she could

grab it. "Remember, this is a secret. You don't want to shrivel up and die, do you?"

"No," whispered Bumble. I slid the cookie toward her again and she snatched it away. Instantly happy, she twisted the sides apart and chiseled the filling with her teeth.

I wasn't too proud of what I had done. But it was for Dad's own good, as he would say himself. The less he knew, the better.

But, just in case, I would watch for the Lizard Man. If I saw him too, *then* I would tell Dad.

That seemed like a foolproof plan.

LAUNDRY DAY

Now that Bumble had put the thought of the Lizard Man into my head, I saw him everywhere I went.

As I waited for Angelo on Monday morning at Mr. Meanie's fence, three cars drove slowly by. With each one I thought, *There he is. That's him.* On Tuesday, a VW van stopped beside me outside the school, and when the door suddenly shot open I leapt away before the Lizard Man could haul me inside. But out came a girl in pigtails, dropped off by her mom, and she looked at me like she thought I was crazy. In third period, I glanced through the window in the classroom door and saw the Lizard Man going by with a rifle. But it was only the janitor carrying a broom.

By Wednesday, I'd made myself so nervous that I didn't want to walk home by myself. So I invited Angelo to come over and play *Alfred Chicken.*

"Sure," he said. "I'll come over after dinner."

"Can't you come now?" I said.

He laughed. "Relax, Watson. It's not that great a game."

I left Angelo at the corner and ran the rest of the way home. At six-thirty, when he suddenly showed up at the front door, I'd almost forgotten that I'd invited him.

On Thursday, with only one more day of school to go, I was doing my very last homework when I heard the shuddering bang of the washer door. Water gurgled through the plumbing pipes.

There was nothing unusual about that. Dad did the laundry every Thursday, and he always slammed the door. But for some reason the sounds made me feel uneasy. When I figured out why, I threw my books aside and raced down the stairs.

I found Dad in the utility room, his back toward the door. He was standing beside the washing machine as it began its cycle.

I said, "Dad."

He turned around and looked at me. In his hand was a piece of paper, crumpled and creased many times. But I could still see the names I'd written there.

"Do you want to talk about this?" asked Dad.

That was what he would call a rhetorical question. I didn't have a choice. But Dad made me wait while dinner was cooked and eaten, while the dishes were done and Bumble was put to bed. I got more and more nervous as I wondered what would happen. Then, at last, I sat beside Mom in the living room while Dad walked back and forth like a lion in a cage.

My piece of paper lay on the coffee table. Every time Dad walked by, it fluttered in the breeze he made, lifting from the table like a moth trying to fly away.

"You couldn't leave things well enough alone," he said. "You had to go poking around, prying into everything. I'm furious about this."

He didn't have to tell me *that*. His face was like smoldering embers, growing redder every moment.

"I told you not to cross Jefferson. But you went where you weren't supposed to go, and you saw things you weren't supposed to see. Who else have you brought into this? Who have you been talking to?"

"No one," I said.

He waved the paper at me. "You thought up this name out of thin air? I don't think so."

Mom tried to calm things down. "We were both surprised by how much you found out on your own. We thought—"

But Dad talked right over her. "How did you get that name?"

"From a directory," I told him. "I looked up the address."

"And how did you know that?"

"I recognized the house."

He crossed his arms and stood with his feet far apart. "I imagine there's more to it than that. I think there's something you're not telling me."

"Look who's talking!" I shouted back at him. "You never tell me anything."

Mom banged her hands on the coffee table. "Stop this!" she shouted.

That brought silence. Mom leaned back and looked at us. "We've been getting along better than ever, and now you're yelling at each other like lunatics. Do you hear yourselves, the two of you?"

Dad was seething. But he gritted his teeth and said, "All right, I'm sorry."

"Now, Igor," said Mom. "What would you like to say to your father?"

She wanted me to apologize too. But I didn't feel sorry about anything. "You treat me like a little kid," I said. *"The less you know, the better. It's all for your own good."*

"There's a reason for that," said Dad.

"Yeah. You're afraid."

Dad seemed stunned. Too surprised to speak, he just stood there turning even redder.

"I've never seen the Lizard Man," I said. "Neither has Mom. All the times you say he's found us, he's never done anything. Maybe he just likes to see you run away. Or maybe it's all in your imagination."

"Igor!" said Mom.

"Well, how do I know it's true?" I asked. "How do I know there are Protectors looking after us? How do I know the Lizard Man is even real?"

Dad looked very sad all of a sudden. Then he closed his eyes for a moment and kind of pulled himself together. "It *is* true," he said. "I wish it weren't, but it is. That man is very, very real."

"So why's he coming after *you*?" I asked.

"As a matter of fact, he's not," said Dad.

That took me by surprise. "Then why do you keep running away?"

"Because he's coming after *you*."

THE REST OF THE STORY

On that summer evening at the very end of the school year, I finally heard the rest of the story—or a bit more of it anyway.

"Perhaps I have kept too many secrets," said Dad. "You were right about the house on the other side of Jefferson. That's where we lived when everything began."

"So why did the Protectors send us back here?" I asked.

Dad looked down at the floor, then slowly shook his head. "I can't talk to you about that."

"Why did you go to the police way back then?" I asked. "What did you see?"

"I'm sorry," said Dad. "I can't tell you that either."

"Why?"

"Because it was so awful that I'll never breathe a word of it to anyone," he said. "I'll tell you only that it happened on the other side of the river, near the bridge, and it involved a man who will almost certainly die in jail because of what I said in court."

A lump bobbed in Dad's throat as he swallowed. "That man's father is your Lizard Man. The night before I went to court to testify against his son, he called me up."

"Oh, it was awful," said Mom. She hugged herself tightly.

"We were all asleep, you and me and your mother. Bumble wasn't born yet," said Dad. "Three in the morning, the phone started ringing. I remember thinking, *This has to be bad news.* Well, I picked up the phone and there he was. As long as I live, I'll never forget what he told me. 'If you put away my boy, I'll put away yours. I'll lock him up in a cold dark place and make sure he never gets out.' "

"You turned as a white as a sheet," said Mom.

Dad nodded. "It scared the living daylights out of me."

Well, it scared the living daylights out of *me* too. I asked, "Will he come after Bumble?"

"No," said Dad. "Only you."

"And what if you think he's found us?"

Dad leaned toward me. "We'll do as we've always done," he said. "If I see the slightest sign that you're in danger, we'll pack up and leave. We'll find somewhere safe and start over."

That made me sick inside. I couldn't stand the thought of moving away. But it was scary to think of the Lizard Man coming after me. What if Bumble was right and he'd found us?

"If he knew where we lived," I asked, "would he come right away?"

"Not necessarily," said Dad. "The Protectors tell me he might watch the house for three or four days. Maybe a week. He would learn our routine, how all of us come and go. He would choose the right time, the right place, and then—"

"No!" said Mom. "I don't want to even imagine this."

But we did. We sat in an awkward silence, all staring off in different directions, all picturing what might happen. Then Mom touched my arm and asked, "Do you have any questions? Anything to tell us?"

"Now's the time," said Dad.

I knew I had to tell them what Bumble had seen. But I didn't want to do it right then. Couldn't I wait till the end of school and Hayden's party? On Saturday, Angelo would come for our last sleepover, and when he went home on Sunday morning I would tell him what was happening. I'd ask him to tell Zoe. Then I'd say goodbye and it would all be over. Just two more days, I told myself. Forty-eight hours, and I'd hardly be alone for a moment.

It seemed safe enough. I would be very, very careful. And for once it would be *me* who was deciding when we were leaving.

So I said nothing.

. . .

Late that night, I lay in bed with my curtains closed to the narrowest slit, watching moonlight ripple on the river. It was just like the old days. I listened for the Lizard Man and tried to stay awake. When I heard Dad coming up to bed I called to him softly. "Dad?"

He opened the door and stepped in, bringing the light from the hall along with him. I blinked and squinted.

The last time my dad had come into my room in the middle of the night—except to drag me out of bed and bug out—I had been a little boy. He seemed uncomfortable doing it now, perching on the very edge of the bed, way down by my feet. He asked, "What's on your mind?"

I didn't want to make him angry all over again, but I had to know.

"What was my first name?"

Slowly, Dad shook his head. "I can't tell you that. The

Lizard Man has never seen you. He has no idea what you look like. But he definitely knew your name, though I don't know how he got it. Maybe from a neighbor. If he called that out and it made you turn around he would know right away that he'd found you."

"But that could happen if he just calls out 'Weaver,'" I said.

Dad looked torn, like he couldn't decide what to do. Then he took a deep breath, and with a sigh he said, "William."

That didn't sound familiar at all. I wondered if Dad had made up a name just to satisfy me.

"We named you William," he said. "After your grand-father. But everyone called you Billy."

I knew that was true. Every part of my body seemed to remember that name.

THE YEARBOOK

There was excitement and sadness as the school year came to an end on Friday. Kids like Trevis, who really hated spending days in class, had begun to remember that *not* spending days in class could be worse. For them, all that lay ahead was two months of sweat and boredom.

For me, there was nothing. Our last day would be a short one, with free period right after lunch as the last class of the year. When I walked out of Rutherford B. Hayes at the end of that period, I'd be leaving the school forever. In a couple of days I'd be gone from the Horseshoe—to where, I had no idea. All the kids I'd come to know, I would never see again.

It made me very sad to think about that, and I tried not to cry.

It was hardest when the yearbooks arrived. They came in three boxes wheeled on a trolley, pushed by Principal Harris. Everyone wanted to open them right away, but Mr. Little said we'd have to wait. "You can pick them up on your lunch break," he said.

I didn't want to be around when everyone got their yearbooks because there wasn't one for me. I'd started school too late to have my picture taken, and Dad wouldn't have allowed that anyway. So I spent the lunch break sitting all alone at the far corner of the field, and I made myself a little late for free period. I had to knock on the classroom door for Mr. Little to let me in.

When it swung open and I saw all the kids in their places, it was just like my first day at Rutherford B. Hayes. Every one of them kept staring at me as I walked down the aisle.

On my desk was a yearbook. I pushed it aside, not knowing whose it was. But as Mr. Little kept talking about report cards, I got curious. I opened the book and found the pages for my grade. They looked like a wall of graffiti, totally covered with writing. It looked like every kid in the class had jotted something there: *UR 2 cool 4 school. Have a nice summer!*

It made me sad and jealous to see those things, and I started to close the book. But my own name suddenly leapt out at me among the scribbles.

Good luck, Igor.

I saw it again at the bottom of the page. *You rock, Igor.* At the left-hand side. *See you in September, Igor!!!!!* And right down the very middle, in the crease of the binding. *I signed your crack, Igor.*

Zoe had written something. So had Angelo, and Trevis, and Mr. Little too: *It has been a pleasure having you in my class.* Even Mr. Moran had added something, though his spelling was never that great: *Play the game, Egor.*

I read every comment; I read them two and three times and forgot all about Mr. Little. Then Angelo nudged my arm and I looked up to see everyone watching me.

"That's a gift from all of us," said Mr. Little.

I couldn't say anything back. I thought I might choke up if I tried.

All the kids brought me their books to sign. They shuffled past my desk in a long line, like I was a famous author or something.

Last thing of all, as I was leaving the room, Mr. Little stopped me. "I just want you to know," he said. "I'm very proud of you, Igor."

THE PARTY

On Friday evening I dressed for the party in clothes that Mom had helped me pick out at Value Village: a white shirt over a black T-shirt, a pair of cargo pants with a hundred pockets. She wanted me to wear a tie. "I'm sure all the boys will be wearing ties," she said.

"I'm sure they won't," I told her.

But she went ahead and got out the tie she'd given Dad in the motel room at Christmas. She held it up like a squashed snake. "You'd look very smart," she told me.

"No," I said. "Please, Mom."

"All right, I won't force you," she said. "But just to satisfy me, would you put it in your pocket? Goodness knows you've got enough of them."

"Okay." I zipped the tie into a pocket of my cargo pants, thinking it would still be there if I ever started school in my next house.

I didn't argue when Mom said she'd drive me to and from the party. I didn't want to be alone if the Lizard Man was anywhere around. As we cruised down Dead End Road, I looked for him among the bushes in the park, between the town houses on the other side. Mom could see I was anxious, but she thought it was because of the party. "Don't worry," she said. "You'll have a good time." And I did.

In the basement of Hayden's place, music boomed from

tall speakers. When Zoe showed up, I didn't recognize her at first. She wasn't wearing ghoulish makeup or glittering jewelry. Instead of her black coat and combat boots, she'd put on a yellow dress as flimsy as butterfly wings. Her shoes had daisies on them.

She stood in the doorway and looked around the room till she saw me. Then she came straight through the crowd, weaving around the people who were dancing.

The music was throbbing with guitars and drums and shrieking voices. I shouted at her, "Hi, Zoe!"

She leaned forward, put her hand on my arm, and bellowed into my ear. "You can't call me that!" Along with her clothes, she'd changed her name. "I'm Catalina."

That was a pretty name. She leaned back and I leaned forward to shout into her ear. "So no more cemeteries?" I shouted. "No more Deadman's Castle?"

"Are you kidding? I'll be up there at midnight," she told me. "Catalina's only here for the party."

Zoe stepped back. Smiling, she held out her hands. "Wanna dance, Igor?"

"I don't know how!" I shouted.

She was already moving her body. It snaked up and down; it wriggled back and forth. Smiling at me, still reaching out, she took two steps backward. Then she whirled away and danced by herself.

It was amazing. The way a movie gangster staggers back while he's been shot by a machine gun, that was how Catalina danced. All around the room she stumbled and lurched.

When the music changed to slow and syrupy, she came

back and pulled me away from the wall. She put her arms around me, and I put my arms around her, and we shuffled back and forth. I leaned my head on her shoulder. Her hair smelled like coconuts and roses.

The song lasted three minutes. I wished it would go on forever, because this was probably the last time I'd see her.

• • •

Dad went to work on Saturday morning. When Angelo came over in the afternoon, I took him straight up to my room.

"There's a weird guy out there," he said.

That sent a shock through me. "Where?" I asked.

"In the park?"

"What's he doing?"

"Feeding squirrels."

"What's weird about that?" I asked.

"It was the way he looked, Watson. Dark suit. Sunglasses."

"Did he have tattoos?" I asked. "Was he driving a big car?"

"I dunno, Watson," said Angelo. "He's probably still out there if you want to look."

I walked over to the corner window, pried the curtains apart, and peeked through the gap at the trees and the bushes. There was nobody there.

"Did you actually see him feeding squirrels?" I asked. "Did he have a bag of peanuts?"

"Give it up," said Angelo. "You sound just like your dad."

I had to laugh because he was right. Dad had made me so fearful that a guy feeding squirrels was enough to upset me. I let the curtains fall into place and got out the Game Boy Dad had given me.

. . .

That night it was hot and muggy. We propped the window wide open by jamming a ruler on top of the box for *Alfred Chicken*.

Smasher lay exhausted on my bed with her three legs sticking straight up. Beside her, Angelo leaned against the pillow and told the same ghost stories he'd told on our very first sleepover. He'd brought his flashlight, and he shone it on his face, and it was all I could do not to tell him I was leaving.

Through the window came a river wind that was warm and wet. Rain showers drummed hard on the little porch roof, suddenly starting and suddenly stopping. Faraway thunder rolled through the sky.

We stayed up past one o'clock. Then, according to our sleepover rules, I curled up on the floor under a thin blanket. Angelo, in his jeans and T-shirt, slipped into my bed. Smasher lay beside him.

I was so tired that I could have slept till noon. But it was still dark when Smasher woke me up with a frantic whining. I banged the bed to get Angelo's attention. "Your dog wants out," I said.

He didn't answer.

"Hey, Bonito!"

Smasher practically *howled*. Afraid she would wake my folks, I said, "Come on, Bonito, let's—"

He wasn't there. The sheet had been pushed aside and Angelo's flashlight lay on the pillow. Outside, the moon was a ghostly circle in a sky full of racing clouds. It dimmed and brightened like a flickering lightbulb.

Smasher was crying at the window. Balanced on her one hind leg, she was trying to leap up to the sill. "Are you out there, Angelo?" I said. But there was no answer.

I crawled over the bed and put my head out the window. "Angelo?"

From down below came a shuffling sound and a muffled sort of cry. Had Angelo fallen over the edge? I imagined him lying on the grass with an arm or leg twisted underneath him.

Smasher was still trying to leap up to the windowsill. She kept falling back on the bed and squirming around to get up on her feet and try again. I put on my shoes, took the flashlight, and climbed out onto the porch roof.

Wet with rain, the ivy was slick and slippery. I grabbed on to the wall to stop from falling, then shuffled to the edge and looked down.

There was a man below me on the moonlit lawn. A dark shape in dark clothes, he was dragging something that struggled and kicked. Like an animal scurrying into its hole, he moved out of the light and into black shadows.

The thing he was dragging was Angelo.

IN THE MOONLIGHT

Smasher kept whining. Down on the grass, the Lizard Man was heading for the bushes and trees at the edge of the park. Hauled along behind him, Angelo writhed from side to side. His mouth gagged, his feet tied together, he tried to wriggle free. But the Lizard Man kept moving steadily into the darkness until both of them vanished into the park.

With a whimper, Smasher leapt through the open window. She hit the cardboard box and knocked it and the ruler loose.

I saw the window closing. Angelo had made it slide so easily that it slammed shut before I could move.

Startled by the sound, Smasher slipped on the wet ivy. She went tumbling down the roof, twisting and squirming, and got to her feet only to fall again. Flat on her belly, she slid backward toward the edge of the roof. At the very last moment she caught herself, and she clung to the ivy by the claws on her front feet. The vines stretched and tightened. The tendrils started popping loose.

I took one step toward Smasher and my foot slipped out from under me. Suddenly I was down on my knees, clutching handfuls of ivy to hold myself there. I saw Smasher looking back at me, her eyes big and pleading. Then, very slowly, she slid over the edge and disappeared.

I crawled up to the window to get back into the house. But the latch had clicked shut and the window wouldn't open.

So I knocked on the glass, banging with my knuckles until I realized it was useless. My parents were too far away to hear me, and Bumble could sleep through anything. To get off the roof I had to climb down.

We could get down here easily, Angelo had told me. *There's kind of a trellis.*

I inched toward it, careful not to slip. I could see where the Lizard Man had climbed up to the window and down again. The ivy was stretched and broken, stripped of leaves in places. I shoved the flashlight into my pocket, leaned out, and clutched onto the vines.

I went down in a rush, like a fireman down a pole, more falling than climbing. But I landed on my feet, and I found Smasher tangled in the vines just above the ground. She clung to them desperately, like she thought she was still ten feet in the air, kicking her one hind leg. I had to pluck her loose and set her down, and the moment her feet touched the grass she went dashing away across the lawn.

She might not have looked like a bloodhound, but she sure acted like one. She raced across the grass toward the bushes and the trees.

The clouds covered the moon, turning everything black.

Somewhere out there the Lizard Man was hidden in the darkness. I wondered if he'd already figured out he had the wrong boy and was coming back for me.

He'll never know. A little voice seemed to whisper in my mind. *Let him have Angelo and he'll leave you alone.*

It was an awful, evil idea. The Lizard Man would never imagine that he'd taken the wrong boy. He had no idea what I looked like. I could let him do to Angelo whatever it was that he meant to do to me, and I'd be free of him forever. There'd be no more hiding from him, no more bugging out.

But I didn't want that to happen. I hated myself for even thinking about it. Angelo was my friend, and I would never abandon him. I would do whatever I could to save him.

The clouds grew thin again, and the moon shone through. I couldn't see Smasher anywhere, but I heard her moving through the bushes. In the darkness beside the house I stood listening for the Lizard Man and watched the clouds stream across the moon. I thought about pounding on the front door until I woke up Dad. But just then, on the other side of the river, the red glow of a brake light appeared. An engine started, and headlights glared white flashes through the trees. Beyond the forest, on a road across the river, a car sped away in a blur of red taillights.

Smasher went crazy. I ran through the bushes and found her barking at the bank of the river. I was sure she'd followed the trail of the Lizard Man right down to the water, and she knew that the car was carrying Angelo away. She *knew* he was gone.

There was no time to get Dad. I had to follow the car. So I picked up Smasher and waded into the river.

The water had risen with the rain. Little waves leapt over my shoes, and with every step I was afraid of plunging into a hole I couldn't see. Smasher wriggled and kicked in my arms, but I held her tightly and set my feet down carefully. If I fell, Smasher would be swept out of my arms and carried away.

When I was halfway across, the moon came out and the

water in front of me turned sparkling white. Then the river grew deeper, and it started flowing faster as I got close to the other side. I slipped on a stone but caught myself and staggered the rest of the way.

As I stumbled up onto the bank, Smasher rolled out of my arms. She fell to the ground with a thud, leapt to her feet, and went tearing off into the forest. I went blundering after her.

She led me up to a street that I'd never seen, through a neighborhood that I didn't know, past darkened houses with everyone asleep. One moment the moon gleamed through churning clouds, and the next the rain was falling again. It pooled on the pavement; it trickled down the gutters.

Smasher kept stopping, sniffing frantically here and there before racing on again. At one dark corner where the gutter overflowed, she lost whatever scent she was following. She stood shivering in the rain, crying like a baby. There was no trail to follow anymore. But I didn't think I needed one. I was pretty sure the Lizard Man was taking Angelo to Deadman's Castle.

A SECRET DOOR

If you put away my boy, I'll put away yours. That was what the Lizard Man had told my father. *I'll lock him up in a cold dark place and make sure he never gets out.*

I wasn't sure I could ever find Angelo down in Deadman's Castle. I'd never gone past the gaping hole Zoe had shown me. But I had no choice. I had to rescue Angelo.

I picked up Smasher. Soaking wet, she shivered and shook in my hands. I tucked her under my T-shirt to warm her against my skin and followed the road to Deadman's Castle. The hill began to loom in front of me.

I walked toward the school I'd known in kindergarten and ached to be a little boy again. I wished the Lizard Man had never come into our lives. The moon darkened and shone again. The rain fell and stopped again. Little bursts of wind made the trees shake like wet dogs, flinging off the raindrops.

On the field behind the school, long tire tracks were churned into the grass. They ended at the foot of the hill where I had sledded in a cardboard box. A big black car sat gleaming in the rain.

Smasher started whining. I felt her heart beating fast against my hand. I was sure Angelo had been in that car— maybe he was still inside it.

I didn't want to go any closer. But I couldn't see the Lizard Man anywhere, so I forced myself to walk toward the car, crouched low as I crossed the open field. All the way, I kept thinking that a door would fly open and the Lizard Man would leap out. The moon brightened, glowing on tinted windows. When I tried to peer into the back, all I saw was my own pale and frightened face looking back. I had to creep up to the front of the car, fighting my old horror that someone would grab my ankles and haul me down from underneath. Then I leaned over the hood and peered through the windshield.

An air freshener shaped like a hula dancer dangled in front of me from the car's rearview mirror. On the passenger's seat was a huddled shape that I thought at first was Angelo. But it was only an old backpack, a heap of canvas and straps.

For the first time since I'd tucked her there, Smasher started squirming inside my shirt. When her little claws scratched my stomach I couldn't hold on to her. She wriggled free and tumbled across the car's long hood. Before I could move she was gone, up the slope and into the forest. I turned on the flashlight and went after her.

The Lizard Man's footprints were pressed into the mud where the hill began. I could see where he had slipped and caught himself, where his hand had touched the ground to keep his balance. There were long gouges that must have been made by Angelo's heels scraping through the mud, and now the tiny prints of Smasher's paws ran right between them.

The Lizard Man knew where he was going. Even where the trail divided, his footprints never backtracked. He had walked steadily, dragging my friend along.

One last burst of rain fell hard through the forest. The sound rushed toward me, and the drops hammered down more heavily than I'd ever seen. But it passed quickly, and then there was a clean, fresh smell that let me know the worst of the storm was over.

The trail became a river. Tiny waterfalls tumbled over roots and stones, digging little canyons in the mud. I had to grab hold of branches to pull myself along, and my feet kept slipping out from under me. The Lizard Man's trail became harder to follow, then disappeared altogether.

I couldn't go very fast, but I was gaining on Smasher. I heard her whines at first, and then snuffled breaths as she searched for a scent deep among the bushes. It seemed she had lost her way in the rain and wandered from the trail. I reached into a thick tangle of bushes to pull her out. And my hand touched cold metal.

There was a door set into the hillside. Maybe four feet high, oval-shaped, it looked like a submarine hatch.

Another way out. I remembered Trevis talking about Zoe. *Once, she went right to the bottom. She found a secret door down there.*

It was made of iron plates turned red by rust, studded with enormous rivets. But there was no handle, no hinge. I shone the flashlight all over it, then started scraping at the dirt. Beside me, Smasher did the same thing, her little claws chewing up the ground.

I felt the metal move.

It was just a tiny tremor through my fingertips. I thought I had worked something loose, but then it came again, a shudder from the metal when I wasn't even touching the door. A flake of rust fell away as something banged inside. Someone was coming out.

I grabbed Smasher and turned off my flashlight. I backed across the trail and into the trees.

With a squeal of metal, the door cracked open. A line of yellow light appeared along the edges of the door. Fingers poked out, curling over the metal. The door opened wider, and out came the Lizard Man.

He looked like a creature crawling from a cave, a hunched-over shape shuffling through the door. He wore a hat like a gangster would wear, and he carried a lantern with a lens as big as a car's headlight. As he turned back to close the door I heard Angelo screaming inside: "Help me! Please!"

His voice was faint and distant, but Smasher twitched in my arms, turning her head. Afraid she would bark, I clamped my fingers around her muzzle. Only a whimper came out of her, but the Lizard Man heard it.

The beam from his lantern slashed like a sword through the dark as he swung it around in my direction.

Already pressed against a tree, I couldn't move any farther away. The light kept sweeping toward me, leaping through the branches, stabbing into the forest. It flashed above my head, moved on and back again, then settled on the door.

The Lizard Man pressed his shoulder against the metal. With Angelo screaming inside, the door squealed shut and closed with a clank.

Still crouched over, the Lizard Man backed out of the bushes. He came so close to me that I smelled his sweat and shaving lotion. Then he lowered his lantern, and the beam lit up the ground in front of him. I was afraid he would look down and see my footprints, and Smasher's, mixed in with his own. But he switched off the lantern, and in the dim moonlight he stood up and set off down the hill.

I took my hand from Smasher's muzzle but didn't move until I heard the car start up and drive away. Then I turned on my flashlight, set it down on the ground, and tried again to get into the castle. Holding Smasher with one hand, I pulled and pushed at the door. But no matter how hard I tried, it wouldn't budge. I picked up the flashlight and climbed up the hill.

At the top, the bricks of the ruined walls shone darkly. Sensing Angelo in the rooms below, Smasher started whining as I started down into the castle. Water plopped from the ceiling, and painted devils seemed to leap from the dark as I swept my flashlight across the walls.

My clothes dripped puddles of water, and my shoes squelched on the hard floor as I walked on through the ruins, past the old mattress, past the bottles with their candle stubs. In the silence of the rooms the trickling of water sounded like laughter and whispering voices. With the hair prickling on my neck, I crept to the edge of the bottomless pit and pointed my flashlight down into nothing. "Angelo?" I called. "Angelo!"

His voice echoed up through the floors, small and frightened. "Igor?"

Smasher yelped and cried and struggled to get free. I shouted at Angelo, "Can you come up?"

"I'm locked in a room." His voice was as faint as a breath of wind. "You gotta come down!"

"I'll go home and get help," I said.

"No!" he screamed. "There isn't time. The guy's coming back. He's gone to get something and he's coming right back!"

I shone my flashlight on the planks that spanned the awful gap in front of me. They were old and cracked, bent in the middle, and they looked far too narrow for me to cross. I felt like this was my last chance to turn back and find someone to help me. If I went any farther I might never get out again.

"Hurry!" pleaded Angelo.

I held on to Smasher and took two tiny steps onto the planks. They twisted underneath me, bending with my weight. I had to force myself across them, shuffling like an old man on an icy sidewalk. As I reached the middle, the planks bent so far that their ends lifted from the concrete floors.

I slid my left foot forward. I slid my right foot forward. The planks rocked and tilted, chattering on the concrete.

My flashlight suddenly flickered. The batteries were running out.

BREATHING IN THE DARK

I couldn't imagine what I would do if my flashlight quit when I was down in Deadman's Castle. It would drive me crazy, I thought, to be suddenly trapped in pure blackness. Again I wondered if I should run back and find help. But I was afraid for Angelo, and I couldn't leave him alone down there.

On I went across those planks, maybe the bravest thing I'd ever done. On the other side of the bottomless pit I groped through the pockets of my cargo pants and pulled out the tie Mom had given me.

It seemed so long ago that she had done that. I wondered how much longer it would be until she found out I wasn't home. Hours would pass before she even woke up. Hours more would go by before she decided the house was too quiet and went up to my room to knock on the door. How long would she wait for an answer?

I imagined her opening the door very slowly, poking her head inside, asking, "Igor? Angelo?" in a whisper at first. Then she would see that the room was empty, and in my mind I heard her screaming.

Dad would go running to see what was wrong. What would happen when he learned that his worst fear had come true?

I didn't want to think about that. I threaded the tie around

Smasher's collar, put her down on the floor, and shouted into the darkness, "Angelo! Call Smasher."

His cry came faintly back. "Smashy! C'mon, Smash!"

Smasher twitched her ears and shot off into the dark. "Keep talking!" I shouted.

Angelo's voice grew louder, then faded again. Smasher pulled so hard on the tie that she half choked herself, and I stumbled along behind her.

"Smash!" shouted Angelo. "Come here, Smashy!"

Deadman's Castle seemed enormous. There was room after room, all alike, every wall sprayed with strange graffiti. But it wasn't until I saw the same leering skull again and again that I realized we were going in circles. Then I found myself back at the bottomless pit, with a flashlight that could barely light up the planks at my feet.

The Lizard Man had left no trail here for Smasher to follow. If there really was a way to get down through Deadman's Castle, I had to find it myself.

I shook my flashlight to make it bright again. I swung it up and down, back and forth, like I was swinging a baseball bat before my turn at the plate. I should have known better. Just as I'd done with the baseball bat, I let the flashlight fly from my hand.

It spun away in the darkness, down through the bottomless pit.

"Oh, no!" I wailed.

Angelo's voice drifted up to me. "What's going on?"

"My flashlight fell in the pit," I told him.

He answered so quietly that I could hardly hear him, in a voice that almost made me smile. "Loser."

I didn't want to go back into the castle without a light. It was my last chance to go home and get help, but Angelo needed me, and I sure wasn't going to try to cross those narrow planks in the dark. Though they lay right in front of me, I could barely see them.

"Come on," I told Smasher. I turned around and started back through the castle, looking for Angelo. With one arm held out in front of me, I groped through the dark like a zombie. I touched a wall and shuffled sideways until I found a doorway. I brushed against cobwebs. I kicked an old bottle and sent it rattling into the darkness.

At my feet, Smasher started growling. I thought the bottle had scared her, until I heard the chattering sound of the wooden planks. Someone was coming in behind me.

I had nowhere to go, nowhere to hide. The clock-like sound of a person walking began to echo from the walls. It got steadily louder, coming closer. Smasher growled again.

I could hear breathing in the dark. Someone was right there in the room, and Smasher's little growls made my blood feel cold. A flame appeared, burning in midair. A voice spoke from behind it.

"What are you doing here?"

I said, "Zoe?"

The flame moved down and I saw her face, a white skull floating in front of me. In her black coat, in the darkness, it was like she was just a head without a body. But Catalina was gone and the old Zoe was back, and I was never so glad to see anyone.

From floors below came Angelo's voice. "Hurry up," he said.

"Are you guys playing a game?" asked Zoe.

"No!" I said. "He's locked up down there."

Anyone else would have asked a million questions and told me, in the end, to go home and call 911. But Zoe only said, "Do I have to do everything around here?" and marched past me.

She let her lighter go out, and in that moment—just inches away—she vanished. I grabbed her coat and held on as tightly as I could. With Smasher pulling at the leash, I trailed along behind Zoe.

"Stairs," she said.

"What?"

My foot went down into thin air. I pitched forward, reaching out to save myself, and found a handrail made of metal pipe. Steep and narrow, the stairs went zigzagging down through Deadman's Castle, down to the floor where the witches met.

"I'm going to use the lighter now," said Zoe. "Watch my feet and don't look at anything else."

The little flame appeared, chasing back the darkness in a circle all around us. It moved along as Zoe walked out of the stairwell, and I watched the heels of her combat boots touch the floor and rise again. I did not look away, but in the corners of my eyes shadowy things appeared and disappeared.

Behind me, Smasher started howling.

"You better carry her," said Zoe. "It's kind of scary."

I picked up the little dog. She buried her face in my arms, her tiny heart beating a million times a minute.

We squeezed through a narrow tunnel and went down another flight of stairs. At the bottom, I heard Angelo still calling for his dog. "Smash! Over here!"

I set her on the ground again. She tried to run but only got caught up by her leash. With a yelp she twisted around, then back again, and popped herself free from her collar. In another moment she was gone, racing away through the dark with her toes clicking on the concrete floors.

"Smasher!" I shouted.

"It's okay," said Zoe. "I think she's heading for the dungeon."

"There's a *dungeon*?" I said.

"Well, that's what I call it. Maybe it was a furnace room or something."

I shoved the tie and collar into my pocket and followed Zoe through echoing rooms. She stopped now and then to flash her lighter and find the way, but we moved through the castle in darkness. Then a yellow glow of candlelight appeared ahead, and I heard Smasher whining sadly.

We came to an iron grate set into the floor. Smasher had her nose pressed through the bars, her tiny tail wagging. The light from the candle shone up from below, casting her shadow onto the ceiling like a huge black bear. Zoe and I looked down through the grate, into a tiny room.

Angelo was standing there, gazing up at us with the most

desperate look I'd ever seen. He looked even wetter than me, and he stood shoeless in a big puddle, with his sodden socks stretched out like penguin feet. All alone down there, he had nothing but a guttering candle. The smell of wax and smoke made me want to sneeze.

Zoe said, "What are you doing in the dungeon?"

Angelo didn't even try to explain. "You've got to get me out of here," he said. "The guy's crazy, Igor. He thinks I'm you. He says I'm going to die in here."

"Who's crazy?" asked Zoe.

"Never mind," I said. "We'll lift the grate and get you out, Angelo."

"Forget it," said Zoe. "It's welded shut."

"Then you gotta come down and open the door!" cried Angelo. "Hurry—I'm scared."

Zoe said she knew the way. But Smasher didn't want to leave. When I tried to pick her up she growled and backed away.

"Leave her," said Zoe. "We'll get her later."

I had no idea where we were. For a guy with a lousy sense of direction, trying to find the way in the dark was hopeless. I just clung to Zoe's sleeve and let her guide me. She was just as blind as I was, but she stopped only once to flick her lighter. She tried to warn me—"Close your eyes"—but I wasn't fast enough.

There was a click, a spark, and then the flame appeared. In a weird and flickering glow, it showed me things I wished I hadn't seen: the curled-up skeleton of a little dog; a leg-hold trap and a coil of chain. I saw a rat scurrying along a twisted pipe, and a message painted in huge letters across the wall: *Beware. The end is near.*

A cold draft pulled at the flame, bending it sideways, drawing out shadows until the skeletal dog seemed to stretch and stand up.

"This way," said Zoe, as calm as ever.

Angelo's little prison seemed as deep in Deadman's Castle as anyone could go. At the very end of a long corridor, it was sealed by a huge metal door.

I pressed my hands against it. I shouted, "Angelo!"

"I'm here!" he yelled back.

I felt the smallest tremble through the door as he pressed himself against the other side. It was all that stood between us, but I couldn't see how to open it.

But somewhere not too far away, with a screech of rusted hinges, another door swung open. The Lizard Man was back.

AN OLD SONG

The distant door opened and closed on creaking hinges. There was a thundering boom as it slammed shut. For the first time in my life I heard the Lizard Man speak.

His voice was an awful rasp that seemed to crawl out of the darkness. "Daddy's home," he said.

There was a *tock-tock-tock* from his shoes as he came walking toward us. He started whistling.

I had heard his song long ago. It took me back to a house I'd forgotten, the music coming from the radio, my mother singing along in the kitchen. But now the Lizard Man whistled only the first few notes, over and over as he walked down that long corridor. *Here Comes the Sun. Here Comes the Sun.*

"Hurry up," said Angelo.

Through the steel door, his voice was barely louder than a whisper. But I was terrified that the Lizard Man would hear him. "Shh!" I said. "He's back."

Tock-tock-tock.

I felt such an awful fear that I couldn't move. Everything my dad had ever told me about the Lizard Man ran in a loop through my mind. *Run away. Scream for help. Never, ever let him catch you.*

He was in no hurry. His shoes made the same steady rhythm.

Zoe moved her lighter up and down the door as we tried

to figure out how to open it. I could see the hinges. I knew it swung out toward me, and not into the room, but what kept it closed? There was a steel rod, a lever, a twisted handle, all lit up one at a time by the flame of Zoe's lighter.

She pointed and whispered, "Try pulling that handle."

It didn't move. But it made a rattling noise that echoed down the corridor, and the Lizard Man stopped walking. He stopped whistling. Zoe let her lighter go out, and in the darkness we listened for each other. It was so quiet that I could hear the tiny tingling of Zoe's jewelry as she turned her head. I even heard her hair brushing against her coat.

The Lizard Man started walking again, faster than before. The tapping of his shoes rang through the castle. *Tock-tock, tock-tock.*

I turned to the door and groped for the lever. Zoe said, "Forget it. We'll wait till the guy leaves again."

"That might be too late." Anything could happen if we left Angelo alone with the Lizard Man. I tried pulling the lever, but it wouldn't move.

Through a doorway, in the dark, the Lizard Man's lantern flashed like distant lightning. *Tock-tock-tock-tock* went his shoes. He was running now.

"Here he comes!" I said. "I can't open the door."

Zoe yanked on my arm. "Let's go!"

But Angelo begged from inside, "Don't leave me here! Please!"

Again I pulled the lever. I used all my strength, but it still wouldn't budge. The Lizard Man's light bounded along the walls, racing closer. "Zoe, help me!" I said.

But she was gone.

The light swung around and pinned my shadow to the concrete wall. Right in its glare, I stood alone outside the door as the Lizard Man came running.

Desperate now, I pulled once more on the handle. Something screeched and something clanked, and the door lurched open. Angelo pushed against it, swinging it toward me. I tried to step back. But caught by surprise, I stumbled and fell, and a moment later the Lizard Man was towering over me.

He looked monstrous, all hunchbacked and twisted. With one hand he slammed the door shut. Then he held up his lantern, blinding me with its glow.

"What are you doing here, boy?" he asked.

I didn't know what to tell him. He swung his foot and kicked me in the ribs.

"Get up," he said.

I rolled over onto my hands and knees, and the Lizard Man grabbed my collar. He was incredibly strong. His fingers squeezed like clamps. He pulled the door open and dragged me into the room.

The lantern glared in my eyes for a moment. Then it swung around the room, over Angelo, into the corners. It reflected off the metal door, and in its glow I got my first good look at the Lizard Man.

PANTS ON FIRE

He wasn't monstrous. He was just a little man wearing a backpack, the same canvas bag I'd seen in the car behind the school.

He was wearing tall boots with checkered pants stuffed inside them, and he looked pretty much the way Bumble had described him. As old as a mummy, he had yellow skin stained with purple liver spots, and a neck like a wrung-out dishrag. From under his black hat dangled strands of white hair.

Up close, the tattoo that I had imagined in such awful detail was just a faded blur on his neck. With a crocodile face and a dragon's tail, it must have looked ferocious once, but now it looked old and harmless, as wrinkled as the Lizard Man.

He held the lantern higher, till its light filled the room. "Billy Weaver," he said.

Hearing that name made me shudder, and the Lizard Man saw it. "So it's true!" he gloated. "Your friend told me I had the wrong boy."

He switched off the lantern. The candle sputtering on the floor was now the only light in all of Deadman's Castle.

"You should have heard him snivel," said the Lizard Man. His voice rose into an awful imitation of Angelo. *Don't hurt me. Please.* Well, I've got the right one now, all right."

I could see past him, up through the grate in the ceiling. Smasher was still there, peering down at us.

"How many years have I waited for this?" said the Lizard Man. "You've been running me ragged all over the country while my boy rots in a jail cell. Well, now it's payback time. You're going to die in here, boy, and your friend along with you."

"Why me?" said Angelo. "I never did anything."

The Lizard Man sighed. "Well, be reasonable. I can't just let you go."

"I won't tell anybody," said Angelo. "I swear I won't."

The Lizard Man laughed. "That's some friend you've got there, Weaver."

"Please!" begged Angelo. "Just let me go!"

"Put a sock in it."

The Lizard Man set down the lantern and took off his backpack. He groped inside it and pulled out a whip, then stepped toward Angelo.

"You ever had a lickin' in your life, boy?" he asked.

Angelo held up his hands. "Don't!"

Smasher snarled. She pulled back her lips and made an awful, sinister growl. The Lizard Man whirled toward the sound.

"Igor!" shouted Angelo. "Eat the feet!"

He was suddenly Johnny Shiloh, and I was Colt Cabana. We leapt from the floor and tackled the Lizard Man. The whip fell from his hand; his hat went rolling into a corner.

"The Frankensteiner!" shouted Angelo.

We knew just what to do; we'd done it a thousand times. With fists and feet we attacked the Lizard Man together.

But it didn't mean a thing. The Lizard Man fended me off with one hand. With the other he knocked Angelo right across the room. In half a minute he'd beaten us both. Then he picked up his hat and his lantern, and he wiped his mouth with the back of his hand.

"Who else is down here?" he asked.

"No one," I said.

"Liar, liar, pants on fire." The Lizard Man switched on his light and shone it up at the metal bars. Their shadows stretched and twisted through the room above. But Smasher was gone.

The Lizard Man put on his hat, covering threads of hair as thin as cobwebs. "See you, boys," he said.

"Don't leave me here!" pleaded Angelo. "Please!"

"You're breaking my heart." The Lizard Man put on his backpack. "*My* boy's been locked up for years. Get used to it."

He stepped from the room. We didn't even try to stop him. Angelo just sat huddled in the corner, looking tiny and sad. The beam of the light shone right onto him until the closing door cut it off and slammed shut. The latches closed; the Lizard Man walked away.

In the yellow light of our dying candle I watched Angelo shake as he sobbed. "Hey, it's okay," I told him.

"Oh, shut up!" wailed Angelo. "We're dead!"

I moved over to sit beside him. I put my arm around his

shoulders, but he threw it off with a shrug. "Leave me alone," he said. "I wouldn't even *be* here if it wasn't for you."

"Zoe's out there," I told him. "She's waiting for the guy to leave. Or maybe she went to get help."

"He'll catch her," said Angelo.

"No he won't."

On the floor in front of us the candle flickered. There was almost nothing left but a tiny wick standing in a pool of wax. Angelo sniffled. "I want to go home."

"We will."

Again I put my arm around him, and this time he let me keep it there. I watched the flame and listened for the closing of the secret door that would mean the Lizard Man was gone. It was a scary thought that Angelo and I would be left in pitch blackness as soon as that wick fell over.

It leaned farther and farther, slowly sinking into the wax. Angelo kept his face buried in his arms and didn't see how the flame shrank, how the darkness seemed to close in.

I thought of the witches, and of the things Zoe didn't want me to look at.

On the other side of the door, the Lizard Man shouted. There were no words, just the sort of grunt that an animal would make. Then somebody screamed—and I was sure it was Zoe.

Angelo heard it too. He straightened up, lifting his head. Outside our room, the latches clicked. The door creaked open.

THE BRAVE LITTLE DOG

In the glow from the dying candle, Zoe's whitened face floated in the darkness.

She came staggering through the door, practically flying into the room. "Hey!" she shouted as she stumbled, sprawling onto the floor. "You don't have to shove me."

The Lizard Man turned on his light and swung it through the room, over Zoe first, over Angelo, onto me. "What a touching picture," he said. "I think I'll just leave you like this."

He stepped backward out of the room and began to swing the door shut. We all must have thought the same thing. Once it closed, it would never be opened again.

Zoe was the first on her feet. She rushed at the door and leaned against it. I leapt up beside her, then Angelo too, the three of us pushing back against the door.

But it kept closing.

We heard a tiny ticking that became the scrabble of Smasher's claws on the concrete. She was coming to find us, running as fast as she could. But the Lizard Man wouldn't even wait to let her in.

"Don't worry," he said. "I'll take care of your little dog."

The three of us together were not as strong as the Lizard Man. The gap between the door and the wall kept shrinking. At the last moment, Smasher lunged through the gap.

She didn't quite make it.

Maybe she just wanted to be with Angelo. But it was possible that she was trying to stop that door from closing. Either way, it didn't matter. The door slammed against her.

There was a thud and a cry that came together, the most terrible sound I'd ever heard. Angelo screamed. Roaring with anger, he lunged at the door. Zoe and I both moved along with him and we hit it together, our shoulders slamming the metal. We drove it back, hundreds of pounds of steel and iron. It crashed into the Lizard Man and knocked him down like a stack of stones. He lay on his back with the beam of his lantern piercing through the dark, shining on a wall covered with the faces of painted devils.

We didn't wait to see if he was alive or dead. Angelo lifted Smasher from the ground, and we raced for the stairs with Zoe leading the way.

Behind us, the Lizard Man stirred. His light flashed along the walls until it shone on our backs. Our skinny shadows, stretched far along the floor, looked like three stick men running on spindly legs.

We couldn't escape that light. It seemed to jump up and follow us, leaping along through Deadman's Castle. Angelo breathed in wheezy gasps, and every time we looked back the Lizard Man was closer.

"This way!" shouted Zoe.

We bounded up the stairs. I heard him running behind us nearly step for step. Around the landings, from floor to floor, his light chased us at every turn.

I stumbled over something soft and rotten, something

that burst underneath me with a whoosh of foul air. Angelo hauled me up and on we went, and again the Lizard Man's light came slicing through the dark.

We were barely a hundred feet ahead of him when we reached the bottomless pit. But we could cross the planks only one by one, and the Lizard Man was coming fast.

Zoe went first. The planks chattered and banged under her feet. On the other side she turned back to help Angelo, reaching out to take his hand when he got close enough. The Lizard Man was gaining on me when I started across.

"Hurry!" shouted Zoe. But I had to go carefully, watching every step. In the bouncing of the Lizard Man's light, the planks seemed to move. They appeared and disappeared as it flashed across them.

On the other side of the pit, Angelo crouched on the floor holding Smasher. Zoe leaned out from the edge, stretching her fingers to grab me. "Come on, Igor," she said.

The planks suddenly shifted as the Lizard Man started across them, just six feet behind me. They bowed like springboards, nearly bouncing me into the pit. I dropped to my hands and knees.

"Hurry up!" shouted Zoe.

I crawled. I moved inches at a time, swaying from side to side like an elephant as my weight shifted from one plank to the other. The ends rattled on the concrete floor, and the Lizard Man was right behind me.

Zoe sat down with her feet in the pit. She leaned forward, reaching out to grab me as soon as I was close enough.

The planks twisted. I started falling sideways. Behind

me, the Lizard Man cried out. I lunged forward, stretching out my hand.

Zoe grabbed it. She pulled me toward her, and I nose-dived onto the floor beside her. In the middle of the pit, the Lizard Man was trying to keep his balance as the planks rocked underneath him. His arms whirled around and around, sending the beam of his lantern spinning crazily across the walls.

With a scream, he fell. The lantern dropped from his hand and went tumbling down in a whorl of light. It hit the wall and went out, and we heard the thudding of the planks as they boomed from the sides of the pit.

Everything landed all at once, what seemed a long time later: the light, the Lizard Man, the planks of the bridge.

Angelo got to his feet, still holding Smasher. I stood on one side of him and Zoe stood on the other side, all as tight together as we could possibly be. We swayed back and forth, until Zoe—with a nervous laugh—said we should maybe move away from the edge.

We made our way through the dark rooms as quickly as we could. Even Zoe was anxious to get out of there, and she led us out onto the hilltop.

There was a golden gleam in the sky to the east, sunrise just minutes away. We looked down at streetlights and traffic lights scattered through the darkness, at a smear of color along Jefferson Street.

Angelo was cuddling Smasher, sobbing as he stroked her head and her back.

"How is she?" I asked.

Angelo's voice broke as he tried to talk. "I think she's dying."

"Let me see," said Zoe.

She took Smasher from his arms and knelt down to set her gently on the ground. The little dog lay without moving, her eyes closed, her tiny teeth still showing in that weird smile. Zoe ran her hands slowly over Smasher's ribs and down her back. The dog's hair smoothed under her fingers and sprang up again behind them. In her long coat, with her black-painted nails, Zoe looked like a witch casting a spell.

"Smashy saved us," said Angelo. "She knew it would kill her, but—" He started sobbing. "But she did it anyway. And now she's dying. She's gonna die."

"Shh, shh, shh," whispered Zoe. She leaned so close to the dog that her breaths moved the hairs on Smasher's nose. "Good dog," she said. "Good girl, Smasher."

Beside me, Angelo put his face in his hands and cried. I held his shoulder.

"You're a brave little dog," said Zoe. "Thank you for saving us."

The edge of the sun appeared in the east, and a burst of golden light shone on the ruins of Deadman's Castle. The highest thing around, it was the first to be lit by the rising sun. For the first time since I'd left the house, I began to feel warm in the sun's wonderful glow.

At my feet, Zoe kept whispering. With her black hair shining, she straightened her back and lifted the dog into the light.

Smasher's head flopped sideways.

THE MEN IN DARK SUITS

I was sure Smasher was dead. The little dog who had saved us was gone. But Zoe kept holding her up to the sky as Angelo blubbered beside me.

"Come on, Smasher," she said.

The glow of the rising sun spread down the hill. It lit up the treetops and the roofs of the houses. It sparkled on Zoe's jewelry and shone in Smasher's fur.

"Come on," said Zoe again.

Smasher's ears twitched.

"Yes. You're a good dog. You saved us."

"Is she going to be okay?" I asked.

"Shh," said Zoe.

She whispered into Smasher's ear. The dog's eyes cracked open, blinked and widened, and in the sunlight they blazed like balls of fire.

"Good girl," said Zoe softly.

Smasher lifted her head. She twitched from end to end and let out a little cry.

"Smashy!" said Angelo.

Zoe brought the dog down and held her close against her heart. She rocked her back and forth, like a mother with a child.

"Let me hold her," said Angelo.

He dropped down beside Zoe. She handed him the little dog.

Angelo and Smasher curled up together in the dirt.

"Careful," said Zoe. "She's hurt pretty bad. She's got broken ribs, I think."

We started down the hill, Angelo carrying his little dog. Without shoes, he had to step carefully over stones and roots. He looked like My Little Pony prancing down the hill. Smasher just lay in his arms, gazing up at him with her eyes wide open. I touched the trees as we passed them.

I still had the woozy feeling that nothing was real. Zoe kept looking at me with worried eyes. She asked, "Are you okay?" and I told her, "Yes, I think so."

It was like she wanted me to keep talking. "You want to tell me what it was all about, what happened in there?" she asked.

"It's a long story," I said. "Remember when we went to the army store, and I took that hundred-dollar bill out of my sock?"

When we reached the bottom of the hill I was still trying to explain everything to Zoe. Just talking about it was a big help, but I was surprised to see that my hands were shaking. Angelo looked just the way I felt, like he was sort of stunned by what had happened. He had been through even worse than me.

"Let's go a different way," he said at the bottom. "I don't want to see that guy's car. I don't want to go anywhere near it."

So we took a different path and came out near the funeral home. The street was empty, and we walked right down the middle, three in a row, the way we'd walked up the hill on my first visit to Deadman's Castle. When we saw a car coming toward us, we moved over to the side of the road.

The car's engine purred as it came nearer. Sunlight shone on black metal, glaring off a hood the size of a Ping-Pong table. The car stopped when it came up beside us. The window rolled open and a man called out.

"Which of you is the Weaver kid?"

Without thinking, I held up my hand as I turned to look at the car.

There were two men inside it, and the driver opened his door and stepped out. He was wearing a black suit with a black tie and shiny black shoes. He said, "Hello, son. We've been looking all over for you."

His voice sounded familiar, but I'd never seen him before.

"You probably don't know who we are, do you?"

It wasn't hard to guess. "You must be the men my dad calls the Protectors."

He nodded. "It's good to see you're safe. Where's our Mr. Griffin?"

The Lizard Man, he must have meant. So that was his name. *Mr. Griffin.* It sounded harmless, even comical, like one of the puppets I'd seen on *Fraggle Rock* when I was young. But it made him human too, in a way I wouldn't have thought was possible only a few hours earlier. Suddenly all the things that had happened seemed unreal, as though I'd only dreamed them.

"He's in the castle," I told the Protector. "I think—"

I choked up. The Protector put his hand on my shoulder and said, "It's okay. We'll take the three of you home. Let you get cleaned up and settled down. Then you can talk to me."

With that, I remembered where I'd heard his voice. He was the man who'd answered the phone when Angelo dialed the number on my hundred-dollar bill.

"How did you know to come here?" I asked.

"Your dad called as soon as he saw you were missing, and we've been looking everywhere for you. Then a man walking his dog spotted Griffin's car in the field and called the police. They let us know."

"But—"

"There'll be time for this later," said the Protector. "Right now I want to get you all home."

"My dog's hurt," said Angelo. "She's—"

"Don't worry, son. We'll make sure she gets help."

The Protector herded us toward the car. He took a black cell phone from his pocket and started dialing. Then he turned away to talk to someone.

The other man got out of the car to open the back door. He was dressed the same way, all in black, and to me he didn't look much different than the first man. But Angelo recognized him right away.

"Hey," he said. "You're the guy who was feeding squirrels in the park."

The man looked embarrassed. "Yes, that's right," he said.

We got a ride home in that big black car, the exact sort of thing Dad had warned me about. With the Protectors in front, Angelo, Zoe, and I sat in the back. Angelo, in the middle, held Smasher on his lap. He kept petting her head and never looked up, never said a word. I thought he was still in shock. But maybe he was ashamed of the way he'd begged and cried. But I didn't know what to say to make things better.

At Zoe's house, the squirrel feeder got out to walk her to the door. As she stepped from the car Zoe said, "I'll see you guys later." Then she bent down and leaned through the window. "Are you going to be okay?" she asked me.

"I think so," I said.

The Protector was back in five minutes. Angelo and I sat almost in silence as we drove back across Jefferson and down Dead End Road. The only thing Angelo said was "So your dad's not crazy after all. How about that?"

I got home to find the driveway packed with official-looking cars. The curtains were pulled wide open in the front window, and Mom and Dad and Bumble stood there, looking out.

The driver kept the car running. "I'll take your friend home," he said. "Tell your parents I'll be right back."

I got out of the car with the other Protector, then turned to look at Angelo. "See you, Bonito," I said.

"Not if I see you first," he said, and I knew at that moment that we would still be friends. Though it might take a while, we could even be better friends than we'd ever been before.

I shut the door and watched the car drive away. Mom, Dad, and Bumble came running out to meet me, and we all hugged each other on the front lawn. Dad looked like a wreck. "I was afraid I might never see you again," he said. "Are you okay?"

"Yes."

He kept his hands on my shoulders, like he was afraid I'd run away. "Are you sure?"

I nodded. "I think so."

"I wish I could say the same," said Mom. "When your father told me you were gone, I nearly died. I really did."

"I'm sorry, Mom." I hugged her again. "The Lizard Man's dead. I saw it happen."

"Oh, honey, I know. They told us already." She leaned down and kissed me. "I'm sorry you had to go through that."

Dad put an arm around Bumble, an arm around Mom and me. "I feel as though I've woken from a nightmare," he said. "I can hardly believe it's over."

I felt him shiver and looked up. He was crying. "Oh, Dad," I said. "You don't have to be afraid anymore."

That made him blush. "I'd better get back inside," he said. "They're giving me the third degree in there."

Mom squeezed his hand as he pulled away. With the Protector still beside us, we watched Dad walk up the path to the house.

"Bumble, why don't you go check on George?" asked Mom.

"Okay!" cried Bumble, and off she went at a run. It made us laugh to see her scampering along. Even the Protector sort of chuckled. But Mom turned serious again.

"You know, it was your dad who told the men where to look for you," she said. "He's come to know that Lizard Man pretty well, and he had a feeling that's where he might have gone."

I didn't know what to say to that.

"He's been looking out for you all along."

The Protector nodded. "I can verify that."

"I don't understand," I said.

"He chose the perfect place to hide," said the Protector. "Surrounded by apartments. People watching every moment. In a crowd, you disappear. We might never have found him if not for your phone call."

I looked at Mom, trying to figure it out.

"Have we been hiding from the *Protectors?*" I asked.

"Yes," she said.

"Since when?"

"Since we came to the city," she said. "It was your father's idea. I didn't want to go along with it at first, but—"

"So he *wanted* the Lizard Man to find us?"

"No, of course not," said Mom. "But the way we were living was tearing us apart, and it had to stop. Your dad thought the safest place in the whole world would be right under the Lizard Man's nose, but he knew the Protectors would never allow it. He made sure that the Lizard Man couldn't get to you without going past him."

"But I messed it up," I said.

Mom smiled. "Not really. You're the one who phoned the Protectors."

"Well, me and Angelo," I said. "But I thought that phone can't be traced."

"It wasn't easy," the Protector told me. "We knew who was calling. No one outside your family has the number you dialed. We got the city pretty fast and the neighborhood three days later. But it was only yesterday we thought we'd found the house. With your dad dressed up, we couldn't be sure. The clown looked suspicious."

Mom put her arm around my shoulder. "Let's go inside," she said. "There's a lot of people with a lot of questions."

"Don't be nervous," said the Protector. "You're the hero here."

When I leaned forward to blow out the thirteen candles on my birthday cake, I couldn't think of anything to wish for. I had great friends, a good school, and a happy family, and that was all I'd ever wanted.

Across the table, Bumble stared at the burning candles. Smoke rose from each one in a little brown coil. "Make a wish, Igor," she said.

But there was nothing I needed. My folks had bought me a computer and a cell phone because Dad said we didn't have to worry about that sort of thing anymore. They'd even bought me a bicycle, because Mom said that every boy should have a bicycle.

But Angelo didn't have one. So I ended up pushing mine along wherever we went, and hardly ever rode it. Zoe thought that was hilarious, like I didn't understand the concept of bicycles. I told Angelo that he could ride it whenever he wanted, but he never did. Trevor said he didn't know how.

"His mom wouldn't let him have a bike 'cause her best friend was killed on one when she was a kid," he told me. That part actually turned out to be true. The part where her friend was hit by the president's limousine, not so much.

"The candles are melting!" shouted Bumble. She kept looking up at me and back down at the cake. "They're going to burn out!"

Still, I couldn't think of a thing to wish for. I was allowed to go anywhere I wanted and stay out until dark, or even later sometimes. And I didn't have to worry about Dad embarrassing me on Jefferson Street. He had quit his job at Fun and Games and was teaching English again.

"Igor!" shrieked Bumble. Her little hands were squeezed into fists, and her eyes were bulging out. "Make a wish!"

I didn't need any money. Dad had told me to go ahead and spend my lifeline. But I'd lived so long with nothing that I couldn't bring myself to break a hundred-dollar bill. So poor Benjamin tagged along wherever I went, still scrunched up in my sock.

The flames reached up like yellow fingers, burning the candles faster. I kept leaning over the cake, smelling the smoke and the melting wax. Bumble quivered all over, and Mom watched me with the cake knife clutched in her hand, ready to start slicing. Even Dad looked puzzled.

"Just make a wish," he told me. "Blow out the candles."

But it wasn't that easy. My last wish had brought the Lizard Man. It had nearly killed me in the end.

It had made me a little bit famous.

One of the big papers ran a tiny story about a man found at the bottom of Deadman's Castle. It made it sound like an accident, and my name wasn't mentioned. Neither was Zoe's or Angelo's, but soon everyone we knew had heard that the three of us were mixed up in it. The story spread from kid to kid like a weird, mutating virus. Everyone got a different version.

Suddenly Deadman's Castle became a scarier place. Kids

still climbed the hill and dared each other to go inside. But no one went farther than the first dark room. They said they heard strange sounds coming up from the bottomless pit.

A month after school had started again I heard that workers had sealed the entrance with metal grates. But I didn't go up to look. Even Zoe had never gone back to Deadman's Castle.

"The candles are falling over!" shouted Bumble.

They had burned to little stubs, leaning in all directions. I had only a few seconds left to make a wish. But I was sure it would come true, and I didn't want to take any chances.

"Bumble, you make the wish," I said.

Her eyes opened wider. "Really?"

"Sure."

Her excited grimace made us laugh. She was so happy that even her hair was vibrating.

"You better hurry," said Mom.

Bumble closed her eyes and bit her lip. She scrunched her face and tightened her fists. "Okay!" she yelled, and leaned forward to blow out the candles.

The flames bent and flickered. Six went out, and then three more. Bumble was turning red.

I helped her. So did Mom and Dad, all of us blowing together. The last candles went out, and the smoke flurried away.

"What did you wish for?" asked Mom.

"If I tell you, it won't come true," said Bumble.

"You could give us a hint."

She thought about that for only a second. Then she grinned. "George is going to be very happy."

AUTHOR'S NOTE

Like Igor, I moved a lot while I was growing up. Before I finished seventh grade, I'd lived in ten houses and gone to seven schools. Like him, I had never had a real friend for any length of time.

But that changed when we moved to Calgary. For three years, we stayed in one place. Our home was an old rambling house that we forever after called "the Yellow House," to set it apart from "the Green House" that came after it. At the bottom of our backyard was the Elbow River, frozen over in the winter, raging brown in the spring with the dirt of the Canadian prairie. On one side was a park, on the other a towering apartment building that shaded the house from the afternoon sun.

To get to school I had to walk up the river and cross a bridge to the other side. I usually used the concrete bridge on busy Fourth Avenue, but sometimes went a little farther to the swinging bridge made of rope and wood.

Behind the school was a hill, and on top of the hill was a ruin that we called Deadman's Castle. It was possible to go down into the ruins, but in third grade I was never brave enough to do that. I had heard that a kid had been killed in there.

Down the street from the school was a funeral home. Sometimes, in winter, we took cardboard boxes from the dumpster behind it and went sledding down the hill, along paths between the trees. I once shot out from a trail and crossed the street so close to a passing car that my brother was sure I'd gone right underneath it.

In all the places we'd known, that was our favorite neighborhood, and it became the setting for *Deadman's Castle*. I imagine it has changed a lot in the fifty-odd years since I've been there, and probably never was exactly as I remember it. I know the house is gone. Condominiums sprawl across the hill that I'd once thought was as tall as a mountain. I'm not sure that I ever want to go back.

This story is, in a sense, a bird's nest of memories. Little bits of my life have been tangled together to make the thing that holds it. In the Green House I was haunted by a man who called me on the telephone. He asked if I'd ever had a good lickin' in my life, then promised to come over and give me one. He always called in the evenings, and only when my father was not at home.

Thinking about it years later, my writer's mind came up with the bizarre idea: What if my father was making those calls?

It's not remotely possible. But that idea hatched in my nest of memories into the beginnings of *Deadman's Castle*.

At first I couldn't decide if the Lizard Man was real or a figment of a madman's imagination. When it was clear that he had to be real, the Protectors had to be real as well. I imagined that Igor and his family would be guarded by federal agents under the Witness Protection Program. But movies and TV hadn't taught me how the program really works. I was wrong.

The real-life Witness Security Program is run by the U.S.

Marshals Service. It provides round-the-clock protection to witnesses and their families, giving them new lives under new identities. And it's done a remarkable job. According to the website of the U.S. Marshalls, not one person under their active protection has ever been harmed or killed while following the program's guidelines.

The Protectors in *Deadman's Castle* are not U.S. Marshals. If they were, the story would not be possible the way I imagined it. I hope people will think of them as guardians, agents of a mysterious and secretive government bureau.